KING OF THE CAUSEWAY

A KING SERIES STORY

T.M. FRAZIER

FRAZIER PUBLISHING

Copyright @ 2020 by T.M. Frazier

All rights reserved. No part of this publication may be reproduced, distributed, or transmitted in any form or by any means without the prior written consent of the publisher, except brief quotes used for reviews and certain other non-commercial uses, as per copyright laws.

This is a work of fiction. Names, characters, businesses, places, events and incidents are either the products of the author's imagination or used in a fictitious manner. Any resemblance to actual persons, living or dead, or actual events is purely coincidental.

Edited by: Karla Nellenbach, Last Word Editing

Cover design: Hang Le

ABOUT KING OF THE CAUSEWAY

As massive hurricane looms off the coast of Florida, a different kind of storm is brewing in Logan's Beach.

A mysterious newcomer is vying for the title of King of the Causeway. He'll do anything to steal the crown, including bringing back someone from King's past who will threaten a lot more than the title King has spent his lifetime building.

A hurricane is coming.

And it could destroy everything.

A NOTE FROM THE AUTHOR

King of the Causeway is a King Series novella featuring King & Doe a.k.a. Ray. Please do not read unless you've read at least King and Tyrant first. Thank you for loving these characters so much that you wanted more, and thank you for being patient with me while I wrote this continuation of their story. I really hope you'll enjoy this novella and are excited for Pike's book because it's coming soon!

For Kebby

And always for L&C

*If you fuck it, let it go. If it comes back to you...
you can fuck it again.*
-Samuel Clearwater a.k.a Preppy

INTRO-FUCKING-DUCTION

PREPPY

Guess who? I'll give you a hinty-hint. I'm as handsome as a supermodel, and as devilish as, well, the devil. I get a hard-on for both pussy and pancakes. I like my blow with a side of blow, and my man meat is enormous.

That's right! It's me, Samuel Motherfucking Clearwater.

If you're wondering how I'm able to do this introduction, then you need to read Bear's story 'cause the end will blow your mind! Then, read my story, you know, because it's about me. I tell you what. If you read it, I'll make you pancakes. Dirty, dirty, delicious pancakes. I'll stand over you and pour that syrup right into your sweaty hot...you get the point.

But, I motherfucking digress.

Basically, I'm here because I'm fucking alive. Like Stefano from *Days of Our Lives,* (Don't pretend like you've never seen it). I just keep coming back for more.

There, you're all caught up on me. Onward and upward, motherfuckers.

I'm going to need you to sit back, hold onto your nipples,

and get ready for the continuation of Boss-Man and Doe's story. Or King and Pup. Or Brantley and Ramie. Shit, between the two of them, they've got like a million names, but it doesn't matter which one you call them, the story is still about the same two people, who just happen to be my family as well as my two best friends.

Important note: Don't tell Bear I said that. That motherfucker will get his titties in a jealous twist if he knew he wasn't my number one man. I mean, sure he plays hard to get, but the shirtless wonder has a soft spot for ole Preppy, and we don't want to go hurting all his big burly man feelings before we even get into the story, right?

RIGHT?

So, relax. Take a bubble bath. Put on some nice calming music like some Offspring or old school Limp Bizkit. Maybe, pour yourself a glass of wine or a light fat joint. A bucket of blow is always a fun option.

Now, for a little recappy cap. *Clears throat*

Once upon a time in a land far, far away, but centrally located in Southwest Florida, was a little awesome, yet shitty town called Logan's Beach. There, long, long ago, two people fell madly in love very much the way most couples do.

It's a tale as old as time. You know, girl with no memory offers herself to boy as a hooker hoping for safety. Boy rejects girl, then kidnaps girl. Then, girl runs away; then boy decides to keep girl. Boy and girl fall in love and have dirty sex and get tattoos. Somewhere in there is a carnival and an incorrect statement about penguins being the only flightless bird. Coolest person in the fucking world dies. Boy offers girl back to her father in exchange for boy's daughter. Girl thinks boy is dead. Girl marries a fucking prick in order to adopt boy's daughter. Boy is actually alive. Girl regains memory and realizes the prick is a super prick. Prick dies violently and much deservedly. Boy and girl get two kids for the price of one in an epic family BOGO.

And they lived happily ever after. The end.

Until now.

Dum dum duuuummmmmmm!

Imma go make me a delicious sammich. Catch you on the flip side.

Enjoy, kids.

CHAPTER 1

RAY

BOOM. Boom. Boom.

Three huge speakers, stacked one atop the other, vibrate and pulse as the music forces itself through them. Deep, bass notes beat against my chest, penetrating my rib cage. My already pounding heart sputters. I cough and wheeze, pulling in a shaky breath. I place my palm over my breast as if it could somehow calm my heart through the layers of clothes, skin, blood, muscle, and bone.

A sheen of sweat breaks out on my heated skin, but inside, I'm ice. Maybe, it's a foreboding. A warning not to take another step.

But I've been through this already.

I don't have a choice.

I choke down my unease with a dry swallow. Each step I take down the narrow hall through the sea of closed-eyed dancers gyrating against one another moves me closer toward the hell I've created for myself.

For her.

I'm so sorry, but I don't see any other way, *I silently apologize to the girl I don't know. The one I was before I lost my memory. The one who took up residence in my body before I woke up on a bench with nothing and became friends with a hooker I don't even like.*

I don't dislike Nikki because she's a hooker, but because she's a bitch.

Through the eerie drug-induced movements of the bodies surrounding me and between the flashes of pulsating light, I manage to keep my eyes trained on the goal.

The door at the end of the hall.

The door to my salvation.

The door to my— a sense of deja-vu breaks my focus.

Wait, I've been here before. I remember all of this.

I know what's on the other side of the door. And it isn't salvation or hell.

It's something way more.

It's love.

It's him.

It's King.

I push my way through the crowd at a breakneck pace, not caring who I knock over or into, and I reach for the handle, throwing the door open and stepping into the dark without the bone-rattling fear I carried with me over the threshold when I entered the first time all those years ago.

"King?" *I ask into the dark room.*

There's no answer, but movement catches my attention. On the bed, a shadow shifts, swinging long legs over the side of the mattress.

I leave the door open and rush to the bed to stand between his legs. I place my hands on his knees. "King?" I ask again, growing worried when my only answer is lingering silence.

After what seems like an eternity, the shadow sits up, his face illuminated from the light of the open door.

I gasp.

King's face is hard and angry and...different. The scar over his right eyebrow that is usually barely noticeable is now raised, cutting a jagged red path diagonally across his nose and lip, ending at his jaw.

"What happened?" I ask. Moving my hands from his knees, I close my fingers over the belts wrapped around each of his forearms.

"Who the fuck are you?" he asks in a deep, gravelly voice. He shakes his arms, freeing himself of my hold.

I search his eyes for recognition but come up as blank as his faded green stare.

"You really don't know who I am?" I ask, hating the trembling words that fall from my lips.

He leans closer, and just when I think he's going to snap out of whatever fugue state he's in that's caused him not to remember me, the corner of his mouth ticks up in an amused smile. "Oh yeah," he says before his smile turns flat. "I remember now."

He stands, and the surprise of the movement knocks me to my ass. He leans over me and grabs my throat, squeezing my airway shut. My sight grows fuzzy around the edges as I struggle against him but it's no use. There's no getting out of his hold.

"You're the one who did this to me. And now, you're going to fucking pay."

As his angry face fades and my vision goes black, I hear myself croak out my final words. "But I love you."

The last thing I hear is the echo of his laughter.

"Pup, wake up. Wake the fuck up!" I hear a scream, and my entire body is shaking. It's not until sleep releases me completely when I realize I'm not shaking so much as being shaken.

My eyes shoot open to find King standing over me much like in my dream. He's got a worried look in his bright green eyes.

He helps me sit up. My breathing is still labored. My body covered in sweat.

"What the fuck was that all about?" King asks, smoothing back my hair.

I blink several times to clear the sleep from my head. King raises an eyebrow. The one with the scar. It's barely noticeable for the exception of the hair to the left of it because it has no pigment in comparison to the black on the other side.

"Pup?" he prods.

I tear my eyes from his scar. "It was a dream."

King scoffs. "More like a nightmare. You leapt off the fucking bed and fell to the floor like you were having a seizure. Scared the living shit out of me."

"The floor?" I look around, and sure enough, I see clear under our bed to the bottom drawer of the nightstand on the other side.

"Yeah, the floor. You were making a choking sound, and for a second, I thought you stopped fucking breathing." He runs a hand through his short dark hair and blows out a breath.

"I'm fine," I assure him, pushing to my feet the best I can. Before I can take a step, King gathers me in his arms and carries me back over to our bed, laying me down gently as if I were made of glass. "I said I'm fine."

He shakes his head. "I know, and I said you scared me," he says, leaning over me.

"It was just a bad dream. I didn't mean to."

"Do you remember what it was about?" King cups my cheek in his rough palm, then rests it on my chest, feeling the pounding of my rapid heartbeat. "Come on. It's not just the nightmare. You haven't been yourself lately. Tell me what's going on in that beautiful head of yours."

"I'm just..." I wave my arms over my belly. "This." It's not entirely the truth. Being pregnant has something to do with how I've been feeling, but there's been something else as well. Something lingering over me like a shadow I can't lose. "Nothing to worry about. Just ate too much pizza before I went to bed. Crazy, pregnant dreams ensued."

King chuckles. "I told you that sour patch kids aren't a great idea for a pizza topping."

"Hey," I reply with my bottom lip stuck out like the child I very much feel like in this moment. "The baby wants what the baby wants."

He nods. "I agree. But maybe, keep the candy and the pizza separate before you turn in for the night?"

Remembering the dream I just woke up from, on the floor no less, I have to agree. "Duly noted."

King leans in over my massive belly and kisses me. The feeling of his full lips on mine sends a full-body shiver down my spine. We've been together for years. Three kids and one on the way, and I still tremble at his touch. They say lust fades with time.

Well, they don't know shit.

King sits up with a groan and runs his hand over his face.

Again, I pout, this time at the loss of contact.

King stands from the bed and holds out his hand to me. "Come on. I want to show you something."

"But, can't you show me later?" I ask, wagging my eyebrows suggestively. "You know, *after?*"

King's gaze rakes over me, starting at my tangled hair, down to my engorged boobs straining against my tank top stained with pizza sauce from last night, stopping at my rounded belly, covered with fresh red stretch marks, which is only half-covered by my all too small top.

No wonder he's turning me down. I'm a fucking mess.

I move my hands to cover my body and look away. I feel my face redden.

He sits back down and takes my hands in his, removing them from my body. "Baby, look at me."

I shake my head like the hormonal, pregnant, petulant child I've become.

"Pup."

I know better than to ignore the warning in his voice.

Reluctantly, I meet his dark green gaze. His forehead is lined, and his lips form a frown. "You don't cover up in front of me. Haven't I said that to you before?"

"Yeah, but that's before I..." I wave my hands at the mess my body has become even though my mind isn't any cleaner. "Before I became *this.*" I hate the lack of confidence in my voice. It's not me. None of this is. It's not my body. My voice. My thoughts. But I can't help the worry, the insecurity, or any one of the negative thoughts I've been having, no matter how hard I've tried to ignore them.

"You don't cover up in front of me. I meant it. You think I don't want these perfect tits in my mouth right now?" King circles my nipple with his thumb, and my entire body jerks as a bolt of pleasure courses through me. His hand moves down my body, over my belly, and cups me over my underwear. He gives me a light squeeze, and for a second, I see nothing but white light behind my eyes. "Fuck, Pup. The way you respond to me." He bites his bottom lip. "You make me so fucking hard. Always have." He leans in, and his lips graze my ear. My skin comes alive with need and anticipation. "With my baby in your belly and everything so sensitive on that fucking body of yours, I'm finding it real hard not to lift you off this bed." He points to the corner of the room. "And make you watch in that mirror as I bend you over, pull on that hair of yours, and fuck you while you scream my name."

My mouth goes completely dry. I swallow hard. "Then why don't you?" Eyes dark with lust, King stands up again, shaking his head. "Because we *can't*." Another wave of rejection is about to crash into me when King adds, "Because of what the doctor said. I can't fuck you. Not until after the baby comes."

"I don't think he used those exact words," I grumble, finally remembering our thirty-six-week doctor's appointment yesterday. I'd had some spotting and mild cramping over the last few days. Everything checked out with the baby, but because orgasms can stimulate contractions and preterm labor, I was given a prescription of no sex or sexual stimulation of any kind.

"So, you *do* remember," King says.

"I remember *now*. Although, in my defense, my thoughts were on the pizza waiting for me at home. I might not have considered the severity of the whole no sex thing."

King smiles. "We've got the rest of our lives, Pup." He kisses me on the cheek and whispers suggestively in my ear, "Besides, I promise I'll spend a lot of time making it worth the wait."

With hard nipples and a throbbing between my thighs that won't be satisfied anytime soon, I grab a pillow from the bed groan into it.

King laughs, and I reward him by lifting the pillow from my face and swatting him with it.

Of course, he catches the pillow before it lands against his chest and tosses it back onto the bed. "Get dressed and meet me in the kitchen."

He helps me up but doesn't release me until I'm steady on my feet. "Wait, what is it you wanted to show me?"

"Meet me in the kitchen, and after I feed you, you'll find out." He heads out the door and shuts it behind him.

"Tease!" I call out.

His response is an echoing chuckle.

The same sense of foreboding I felt in my dream snakes its way up my spine. I shudder as a shiver wracks my body.

I tell myself that the feeling is probably just a result of the nightmare or the sometimes overwhelming anxiety I've been experiencing lately or the pregnancy hormones or the lack of a morning orgasm or any of the other thousand things that could explain the sense of doom I feel deep in the marrow of my bones.

Or maybe, it's something much much worse.

CHAPTER 2

RAY

"THIS HOUSE IS GONNA BE FUCKIN' epic after the addition is finished. Wish I thought of it when I still lived here. Remind me, did you guys decide yay or nay on my red room suggestion?" Preppy asks. He hands me a bowl of popcorn and plops down on the couch.

I toss a kernel at Preppy.

He catches it in his mouth. "I'll take that as a no. I should've known ya'll were a bunch of prudes."

"Oh yeah? Where's your sex dungeon? Because I don't remember seeing one in your house the last time we were over."

He raises his eyebrows. "Are you kidding me? If it wasn't for the kids and that whole inappropriate thing Dre keeps reminding me about, I'd have a whole sex *house*."

King showed me the progress being made on the addition to our house this morning. It's all framed out now and ready to become a new master suite, additional bedroom, kitchen expansion, and big sound proofed playroom for the kids. It will take a few more months to complete, but Preppy's right. When it's all done, it's going to be amazing and provide our growing family some much needed additional space. No red room. Although, now I'm thinking about sex again. Or the lack thereof.

Like I need more things to feel frustrated about right now.

"What the fuck is going on with your face?" Preppy asks, leaning in and squinting to get a better look at me.

I cover my face with the blanket, and he pulls it back down.

"I mean it. Why you frowning? Boss man ain't laying the dick down like he used to or something?"

"Or something," I mutter, popping a few kernels into my mouth. It doesn't help.

It's not King. Or sex. Or sex with King.

Which is a problem, but it isn't *the* problem.

Preppy chomps on another handful of popcorn. "You know, they make medicine for that now. Say the word, and I'll get your boy some shit that will make his dick into a fucking shuttle launch."

I sigh and make sure the gaggle of our combined kids aren't listening. They aren't; all six of them are engrossed in the movie currently playing on the tv. "No. He doesn't need drugs. At my most recent doctor's appointment, they put the smack down on our sex life until the baby is born."

"You mean until six weeks after the baby is born," he corrects.

Fuck. I forgot about the wait time. "Thanks for the reminder."

He tosses a popcorn at me and it lands in my hair. "Anything to assist you with your sexual frustration. When Dre had the twins, that was a rough six weeks. Gave myself dick-rope burn."

"How did you get..." Understanding dawns on me. "Never mind. I get it." I lower my voice. "But so much that you gave yourself rope burn? Really?"

"Yup." He turns to face the TV. "Didn't help that I used a rope." Preppy's face turns serious. He nods. "Yeah, with a rope."

Time for a subject change. My thoughts turn to this morning's unsettling weather report. "I just wish this storm would pass so we could keep going on the construction."

Preppy waves his hand in the air like he's sweeping my worry away. If it were only that easy. "It's a baby storm. A cat one or two. It's not even supposed to make landfall. It will swirl around off the coast for a few days and make its way toward its final destination and unfortunately some other undeserving town."

"Is that supposed to make me feel better about it?"

"Take it up with Mother Nature," Preppy responds. He raises an eyebrow suggestively. "But think of how happy you'll be rubbing one out in your new clawfoot tub if it makes you feel any better."

I chuckle. "Yeah, masturbating in my new tub makes me feel much better about the potential catastrophic destruction of a town and possible loss of life."

"Then, my job is done here. You're welcome."

I think of all the work King has put into making my drawing for the new rooms of the house a reality. The man really would stop at nothing to make me happy.

You won't be happy. Not in the tub. Not anywhere. You

can't be happy. Not anymore, the voice inside my head taunts. The one that fills me with needless yet endless amounts of worry and doubt.

I will the voice away. Whatever this is looming over me is just like the storm lingering off the coast. It's temporary, and it will pass. It has to pass. Besides, I have love, and therefore I have everything.

And that love comes in all shapes and sizes. Romantic love like the kind I feel for King comes with passion, attraction. Parental love comes with a need to protect, a deeper love than any in the world. Then, there's the kind of love that comes in the form of friendship. Chosen family. Currently, it's in the form of the blond, tattered and scarred, tattooed man snuggled under a soft blanket on my couch, who is currently mindlessly rubbing my swollen feet.

"Mommy, what's mastered-batoning?" Max asks, looking over her shoulder.

"You mean masturbating," Bo replies before the shock of my daughter's question has a chance to set in. "Also referred to as self-pleasuring. It's the stimulation of the genit—"

Preppy claps his hands together. "Okay! That's enough of that. Are you ready guys? This is the best part!" He points to Bo and whispers, "No more listening to adult talk."

Bo shrugs. "Then, don't adult talk in a room full of kids. Or, and this is merely a suggestion, but you both may want to consider working on the volume of your whispering."

Preppy opens his mouth to reply, then shuts it. He purses his lips, then settles back on the couch. "Touché."

Sammy, Max, and Preppy's twin girls, Taylor and Miley are all lying on the floor on their stomachs while Bo opts for the recliner. Nicole Grace is on the floor, too, but she's already asleep with her purple blanket shoved in her mouth in a way that used to make me think she was trying to choke herself.

"Here it comes!" Preppy points to the TV, and the kids all clap with excitement as Moana begins to sing her first song. Preppy sings along, and the kids follow.

I smile at my friend who is a literal juxtaposition of a character. Loving yet foul mouthed. Sexual and crass but loyal to the wife he's hopelessly in love with. A party animal but one of the best fathers I've ever witnessed. When the song is over, they all clap and continue to watch the movie.

"What?" Preppy asks when the song ends and he catches me staring at him.

"You're a good guy, Preppy," I say, because I mean it. Grace was right all those years ago. It's possible to be a bad boy yet a great man. I'm lucky enough to know and love several such men and call them my family.

"You're only saying that because I'm currently rubbing your pregnant Flintstone feet."

"Hey," I chide, lifting said Flintstone feet from his lap.

Preppy rolls his eyes and pulls them back, continuing my much-needed foot massage. "Dre loves the shit out of me, but I have no doubt that she loved me even more when she was pregnant. I'd spend hours robbing her cute swollen feet."

I shake my head. "I'm saying you're a good guy because you are."

He shrugs. "I'm good-ish, or like good adjacent. Maybe. Possibly. Probably not."

I smile. "That sounds about right."

"Daddy?" Taylor asks turning around and staring at us with her huge doe eyes and cherub cheeks. "Moana is brown, right?"

Preppy's eyes grow wide. "Oh, yeah, I guess," he answers

with a *where is this going* look in his eyes that as a parent I am all too familiar with.

"And I'm white, right? " she asks, tilting her head. A little black tendril falls over her eye, and she blows it away only to have it fall right back.

"Uh, huhhhh...," he replies, shifting his eyes to me, then back to one of his twins.

Taylor smiles up at her daddy. "But, we're all the same inside, right?"

Preppy blows out a sigh of relief and smiles down at his darker-haired twin daughter. There's pride in his voice. "Yeah, kiddo, we're all the same inside."

Satisfied, Taylor turns back to face the TV while Preppy stores at her for a few silent moments before speaking again. "You never hold your breath until the moment when you think your toddler is about to come out to you as a racist."

I chuckle. "Well, you're doing something right. She's barely three years old and has recognized that although people might look different, we're all the same. She's smart. Observant. Kind."

"She gets all that from her mother," Preppy says, clearing his throat, clearly uncomfortable with the compliment. Which is very unlike him. Normally, he leaps at the chance to accept a compliment like he's receiving an Oscar.

I press my foot against his still hand, and he resumes rubbing my swollen feet. "Give yourself some credit for being a decent human."

He smirks.

I roll my eyes. "A decent human, *at times*."

"A reminder that you're the one who pushed King and I

together when we did everything in our power to pull ourselves apart."

"Pffft, the two of you were so perfect for each other, you could be blind and deaf and still know you were meant to be."

"I think there's more to it. I think you knew we'd be happy. That *he'd* be happy."

"That, or I just didn't want you to leave so I made sure you'd stay. It's more selfish than you're making it out to be."

"Uh, huh. You keep telling yourself that, Prep. Meanwhile, you're here rubbing my feet and watching Disney movies with the kids. But I promise, your secret good parenting and being a good friend is safe with me."

"You know I love me some motherfucking Disney," Preppy replies.

"I love me some motherfucking Disney, too!" Bo chimes in, repeating his father's words. He's the only child not sitting on the floor. Instead, he's sitting with his legs crisscrossed on the recliner wearing a pink and yellow plaid bow tie that matches Preppy's.

Preppy tries to hide his crooked smile and narrows his eyes at his son. "Bo, what did we say about using those kinds of words?"

Bo recites his answer without apology, like he's remembering them from a textbook. "Not to say them in front of my mother, my sisters, or my teachers because they don't understand that swearing is a sign of emotional intelligence according to recent medical psychological studies in major publications. And socially not acceptable for an eight-year-old to use in public because it makes mom look like she's not doing her job when we all know that my terrible language is all your fault."

Preppy nods. "That's right."

Bo points to the TV. "But Disney movies *are* motherfucking awesome because behind all the singing and princesses, they're really morbid. Did you know that Moana is one of the few Disney movies where the parents don't die in the beginning? Although the grandma kicks it, but then, she becomes a stingray, so that's pretty awesome."

"Yeah, it is pretty awesome," I reply. I look from Bo to Preppy. "You know, he might not be your blood, but he is so your kid." I chuckle. "In every way."

"Yeah, yeah he is. But, he's smarter than I'll ever be," Preppy says, staring at his son.

"I think he's smarter than any of us will ever be," I add.

Bo takes a handful of popcorn and shoves it into his mouth. "That's true because my IQ is one fifty six. Technically, I'm smarter than 97% of the population will ever be." He turns back to the movie.

"He's right. We need to work on our whispering skills," I whisper as low as I can manage. "You know, it's crazy seeing you as a dad, Preppy. Do you ever miss the way things were before you had kids?"

Preppy frowns. "What? Like do I miss having sex with anyone and anything in any manner of my choosing without giving a fuck if it's wrong or right or demented?"

"Something like that."

"Nope. And let's face it, in most ways, I'm still the same ole me. I'm married, but that doesn't mean that I don't find most bitches—I mean, women—sexy as fuck anymore. And it doesn't mean that I still don't want to do horrible, deplorable, dirty—"

I cut him off. "I get it."

"The only difference is that now I only want to do those things with Doc." He looks to where the twins are both asleep on their stomachs next to the equally passed out Max and Sammy, then back to Bo, who has a notebook on his lap, scribbling in the pages. "You already know I didn't have a family growing up. Now, I get to be in one. My only goal is not to fuck them up too much and let them be themselves."

Tears well up in my eyes. I try to hide them by turning back to the tv while willing them away.

Preppy pauses his hands on my foot. "You okay, kid? You seem a bit off, and I'm an expert at sexual frustration, but this seems like something else. You normally laugh when I say stupid shit, and now the laugh either isn't there or...I don't know, just not what it used to be."

Great, another person that's going to be asking me if I'm okay every twenty minutes. I force a smile. "I'm fine. I really am. It's just a sweet movie. And you know, hormones and shit." I sniffle.

Preppy's frown says bullshit, and I can feel his gaze penetrating my façade through my temple. "It wasn't that sweet. And I'm not just talking about today either. You've been like this for a while now."

"Like what?"

"Like your best friend died, but I already did that so...what is it?"

I don't answer because I'm not sure how to answer. The same reason I haven't explained it to King. How can I explain to them a feeling that I don't quite understand myself? Plus, I know how heavy the weight of worry feels, and I don't want to pass it off to them and have them concerned about me when I'm not even sure there's a reason to be concerned.

Preppy snaps his fingers. "Wait, I know. You didn't laugh as much because you're afraid that you're gonna pee. That happened to Dre when she was pregnant and laughed too hard. A little after she was pregnant, too. She was embarrassed, but I didn't mind. I actually kinda like it when—"

"It's nothing," I blurt, not wanting to hear the end of that sentence although mentally I've already heard it all. "I've just been a little tired."

He doesn't look convinced. "You sure?"

I smile and try to make it as genuine as I can muster. "I'm sure. Plus, pregnancy mixed with exhaustion equals emotional. I'll be fine tomorrow."

"I tell you what. You go to bed, and try to rest. I'll finish the movie with the kids, and I'll wait for boss man to get home before we head out."

I'm about to argue with him when he insists. "Bed, kid. Now. If not, I'll have to consult with that barbarian of a husband of yours, and you'll be accosted with the Brantley King edition of the inquisition until one or both of you dies from mental exhaustion."

I don't want to have the same conversation with King again. I don't like lying to him, but I am fine. Or, I will be fine.

Or I hope I'll be fine.

I concede to Preppy's offer and maneuver my huge belly so I can shift to the side and stand from the couch. "Thank you."

I'm halfway down the hall when I hear Preppy. Again, Bo was right. He does need to work on his whispering skills. "Okay, kids. She's gone. Who wants some cocaine?"

I look over my shoulder and find Preppy silently laughing at his own joke. "They're all asleep," he continues, pointing to the floor. "And you, of all people, know I'd never give my blow to kids. They ain't got no money or collateral."

CHAPTER 3

KING

MY HANDS MAY BE SLIGHTLY CLEANER these days, but my cash is still dirty as fuck. And at this moment, someone is trying to fuck with what's rightfully mine. What I've spent two decades building in this town.

When it rains, it fucking floods.

I'm not talking about Hurricane Polly, either, although that's not exactly helping matters.

The latest shit storm was last night. Nine and Pike, along with one of Bear's guys they call Badger, were moving a shipment of blow when it was jacked on the middle of the fucking causeway. MY fucking causeway, by some wannabe thugs for hire.

Unluckily, I'm the one who fronted the fucking cash. Like I need more shit to be worried about right now in addition to Pup and whatever the fuck it is she's keeping from me. I'm somewhere between angry and confused that she's not being honest with me, and I hate to fucking admit, hurt.

Which just makes me even more angry.

I step into the framed addition to the house. Pup really did draw up a great plan. When it's done, it will be a new master suite, a kitchen addition, and a huge playroom for the kids. What Pup doesn't know is what else it will include, but I plan on holding onto that bit of information from her until its complete and every room looks just as she's imagined.

Currently, it's just a place that smells like sawdust—I spy Pike and Nine waiting for me inside the framed walls—and bad fucking news.

Pike is mindlessly twirling his handcuff bracelets around his wrists with his back against one of the studs. His chin-length beach boy hair falls into his battered face. There's a cut above his right eye and a blood stain where he's bleeding through the bandage. There's a bruise under his other eye.

Nine is on his phone, but looks up when he hears me approach and shoves it back into his pocket. I consider the kid my protege, and not just because he's Preppy's brother, but because he's smart as fuck, violent when the situation calls for it, and willing to take direction. He's the next generation. The Prince of Logan's Beach.

If he doesn't fuck it up before he even gets started.

Nine, as usual, doesn't waste any time getting down to business. He turns over a neon orange bucket and takes a seat.

"Tell me everything." I demand. "What the fuck have you found out?" I light a smoke to give my hands something to do besides tear down the wood surrounding us and breaking it over my knee.

Nine sighs. He's got a busted lip and a red mark on his cheek. "We're on it, but not much luck yet."

It's the last thing I wanted to hear. I take a step toward him and feel the vein throb in my forehead with each step. The chords in my neck tighten. I lean down and point my smoke at Nine. "*Nobody* fucks with us in this town. That's rule number one, and whoever is behind this is going to learn that the very fucking hard way.:

Nine doesn't shy away from my order. He seems to embrace it. Gain confidence from it. As does Pike.

Nine's shoulders straighten, and he nods.

I turn to Pike. "Don't fucking stop looking until you've talked to everyone in this town, until you've turned over every grain of sand on that fucking beach. Don't stop until you have a name or, better yet, a body."

Nine stands. "You got it, Boss."

I almost feel bad for the kid. He knows what to do and what his job is, but I'm too angry right now to muster up false fucking politeness for the sake of his feelings. "So, what do we know?" I ask, taking a step back and trying to fan the flames of my boiling blood.

Pike steps away from the wall and wrings out his hands. "We know that fuckers were wearing masks. Skeleton ski masks of all things. They didn't sound or look familiar. If you ask me, they're hires and not affiliated. The way they jacked us was reckless and not well planned. They shot up the truck tires from behind the guardrail, and we crashed into the median. They surrounded the truck before we could fire back and ordered us out of the truck. When Badger told them to go fuck themselves, they shot him."

"How he holding up?" I ask. I don't want anyone to die on my watch and in my town. Not if I can help it.

Pike shakes his head and lights a joint. "It was a through and through. We got him over at Nurse Jill's spot. He's on a half a bottle of Jack and some blues. He's been whistling dixie for the last six hours. Literally. So, I'd guess that it's safe to say he'll be alright. Well, after the massive hangover I suspect the fucker will have.

I nod. "You said they didn't sound familiar. So, what did they say?"

Pike hesitates and turns to Nine. "Tell him."

Pike blows out a breath. "One of them said to tell you that there's a new King of the Causeway in town, and he'll take everything from you, unless..." He looks as if he's about to take a bat to the dick the way he holds his breath.

"Unless what?" I ask, feeling the tendons in my neck strain. "Out with it!"

His eyes meet mine. "Unless, you give him what he wants."

"And what the fuck is that?"

"I asked the same thing. He said you'll be finding out soon enough." Nine reaches up to his forehead and touches the angry red knot right below his hairline. "Then, he used the butt of his gun and knocked me the fuck out."

"Hack into every security camera from here to fucking Miami. Find out where that fucking truck went. Pike, call up every blood-sucking connection you have from street dealers to the cartel. Get me a fucking name. And when you get one." I take a deep drag. And blow the smoke out slowly through my nostrils like the angry fucking dragon I feel like right now. "You call me first."

"On it," Nine replies with a curt nod.

I leave with rage coursing through my body. Every muscle strained and tense. Whoever is behind this will pay the old-fashioned way. The way I built my name and my business.

In fucking blood.

. . .

I head up to the part of the house that doesn't consist solely of dead trees and not much else. I half-expect the kids to run out like they usually do when they hear me coming up the steps, but there's no one greeting me today.

Inside, I find my living room full of sleeping kids, both mine and Preppy's. The only exception being Preppy himself who is wide awake and intently watching whatever singing cartoon is currently holding his attention.

I open the fridge and grab two beers. Preppy hears me and looks up. He stands from the couch and jerks his chin toward the back door. I wait by the door and hand him a beer, following him back outside. I slowly shut the screen door so I don't wake the kids but keep the interior door open in case one of them wakes up.

"Where's my girl?" I ask, taking a swig of my beer.

When we reach the grass, Preppy lights two smokes, handing one to me. "I sent her to bed. Well, I sent her to bed after giving her a famous Preppy foot rub."

Instinct has my knuckles turning white even though I know Preppy is no threat, but when it comes to my wife, I can't help the rage I feel when it comes to another man touching her, no matter how innocently.

"You're so cute when you're all jelly," Preppy comments, staring at my clenched fists.

I roll my eyes and ignore the instinct to beat the smirk off his face. The kid has been through enough in the last couple of years. He doesn't need my baseless wrath. At least, not today. And he is my best friend, although my blood pressure currently thinks otherwise.

The sun's last rays of the day beam through the mangroves, and I realize how early it is. "Wait, she's in bed already?" I ask, concern crawling up my spine like a spider making its way back to its web. Even pregnant, Pup isn't the sort who takes breaks, even when they're much needed.

Preppy takes a deep drag and shrugs, the movement constricting a deep jagged scar on his neck. "She says she's tired, but if you ask me, the kid don't seem like her usual herself."

I see my concern mirrored in his eyes and I sigh out of pure frustration. "Yeah, I know. Every time I ask her about it, she tells me she's fine."

"She's stubborn as hell." Preppy quirks an eyebrow at me. "Reminds me a lot of her husband."

"Even so, it doesn't change the fact that I still don't know what the hell's bothering her, or better yet, why she feels like she's got to lie to me about it." I've been stabbed and shot, but my wife not feeling like she can be honest with me hurts a fuck of a lot more than a bullet piercing through skin and muscle or a jagged blade jutting against bone.

"Tell me this, Boss-man. Why does anyone in a relationship, one where they actually like the other person, lie to their partner?" he probes.

I'm too worried about Pup to try to answer a riddle right now. "Why?"

Preppy stubs out his smoke. "Ugh, you're hopeless. She's trying to protect you, you fucking caveman. Why else?"

"Protect me?" I scoff. "From what?"

He crosses his arms over his chest and leans against the banister of the stairs leading to the back door. "Let me put it this way. If she told you what's really wrong, what's the first thing you would do? Be honest."

I shrug. "Easy, I'd fix it."

He makes a finger gun and points it at my chest. "Bingo."

"What the fuck does that mean?" I growl.

"It means that maybe what she's going through can't be fixed with a punch to someone's jaw or a bullet to someone's head."

"If it could only be that easy," I mutter. I look down to the belts I wear wrapped around my forearms.

Preppy laughs. "Okay, or a belt around the neck. Whatever your girl is dealing with, she obviously thinks she needs to go through it alone because she doesn't want to bother you with it. Or anyone else for that matter."

"So..." I pause waiting for Preppy to say something. He doesn't. "So, what the fuck do I do?"

He shrugs and takes a drag of his smoke. "Not sure. Maybe, you make her realize she's not alone. That you're not going to just try and fix it, but understand whatever it is."

Preppy's right, and it grates on me like a rope chafing my skin. "When did you get to be so smart?"

He takes a dramatic bow. "Death has a way of giving someone new perspective on shit. Things I never thought I even had an opinion on before. Like, don't get me started on Oprah's book club choices. Mainstream bullshit sponsored by a failing pub—"

"Do me a favor, Prep?" I ask, stubbing out my own smoke.

"Yeah, Boss-man?"

"You're smart enough, so don't go dying again. You being brilliant would be even more fucking irritating."

Preppy claps me on the back and follows me back into the house.

"It's a motherfucking deal." He lowers his voice to a whisper. "What the fuck is going on with the shipment? Any word on who the fuck is involved?"

I shake my head. "No, but I'm gonna find out."

Preppy cracks his knuckles. "Good, let me know when you do." I see his eyes widen along with his smile when an idea passes over his face. "I've got the best idea ever."

"Fuck, do I even want to know?"

"After you find out whose fucking with you, I know where we can take him. It's been a while and I might have to spruce it up a bit, but it's been way too fucking long. I'll give you a hint. Three words. One of my favorite places in the world."

I feel a smile spreading across my face. I can't help but share in his excitement of what's to come and where.

The Killin' Shed.

CHAPTER 4

RAY

A FEW DAYS LATER...

Our kids are chasing each other yet again. The little one is crying because she can't keep up with the big kids. The one in my stomach is doing somersaults. Preppy is here again, but this time without the kids because his wife Dre took them to New York for a visit with their grandfather. They're supposed to come back the day after tomorrow, but Preppy told them to be prepared to stay longer in case the storm shifts direction, which tells me he's more worried about it than he led me to believe.

I'm pretty sure King has placed Preppy on babysitting duty (me, not the kids) while he's trying to figure out the situation with the shipment. I wish I could do more to help, and I hate seeing King so angry although I know he's been toning down the severity of that anger when he's around me and the kids. I don't mind Preppy being around. He's been a much-needed help and distraction.

Art, tattooing used to be that distraction. I've come into my own over the years when it comes to design and ink. I itch to get back to it, but even if I wasn't hugely pregnant and unable to sit in one position for an extended period of time, I haven't exactly felt inspired. It's been months since I picked up a tattoo gun or a pencil.

I'm cleaning up a broken remote for the tv, popping the batteries back in when King walks in the door and takes it from my hand.

"Who did this?" he asks, raising an eyebrow toward the kids.

"One of them that isn't currently occupying space inside of my body." I point to where all three kids are suddenly still on the couch. The picture-perfect trio of innocence smiles up at their daddy.

"Devils. All of them," Preppy mutters from the kitchen. He points his pancake spatula at his own chest. "And for the record, it wasn't me."

"Sorry I took so long. It took me half an hour just to get from Bear's club to the Causeway. Then, I had to turn around."

"Why?" I ask.

"A boat crashed into one of the pilings. Did so much damage that they had to close it down."

"Until when?" I ask. The Causeway is the only way on or off Logan's Beach by car. I'm due in a few weeks, and the hospital is on the other side.

"I guess until they fix it. The worker who told me to turn around said might take up to a week."

I feel a rush of relief wash over me.

King leans in and kisses my forehead. "Already thought about the hospital. That's why I asked."

He reconnects the remote pieces, tucking the batteries back inside and points it at the TV. He changes the channel to make sure it works and sets it down just as the weatherman from our local station clears his throat. "Good evening. I'm meteorologist Dexter Greyson here with a Hurricane Polly update. I know we were expecting category two winds at most with the category three winds staying more off the coast and up in the Port Charlotte area. Unfortunately, as of the 5am hurricane center update, not only has Hurricane Polly made a drastic turn south far from the forecasted cone, but it's also picked up speed and strength. We are now expecting a landfall in the Logan's Beach to Coral Pines area, today in the early evening hours. I'm sorry to report to the residents of Logan's Beach that with the bridge unpassable and the waters already unsafe for travel by boat, that taking shelter in the highest, most sound structure is the most advisable course of action." The harried-looking weatherman pauses to take a sip from his Channel Two mug. "Stay safe, and may God be with you all."

I have no idea where to start. I sit down because my head is dizzy with jumbled thoughts. *Will the kids be safe? Will we be safe? What about the house? Flooding? Our insurance? Power? Where is the generator?*

"Breathe," King orders, placing a hand on my shoulder. I cover it with my own. "It'll be fine."

Preppy shrugs. "It's nothing we haven't been through before. Besides, the dude from the weather channel isn't even in town, and everyone knows that the only time to worry is when he shows up."

The news anchor once again throws to the weatherman. "Just an update, and I hate to be the bearer of bad news, but I have a report in that Jim Cantore from the Weather Channel has been spotted broadcasting from the bottom of the Causeway."

"Fuck," Preppy swears.

"Really, of all the things he said, that's what bothers you most?" I ask, pointing to the TV.

To my surprise, King comes to Preppy's defense. "Cantore goes wherever is considered ground zero during a storm."

"What are we going to do?" I whisper to King, cognizant that the kids are watching us and not wanting to make them as fearful as I am.

"We are going to get through it," King says, as if it's as simple as that. I believe him because I have to believe him. Because I can't imagine a world where any of us don't get through it.

The reporter continues as the kids chase each other down the hall. "Although the winds will be a big factor in this hurricane, flooding will be the major concern for our area as we are on the low-pressure side of the storm. Get to high ground and an internal room to avoid flying debris. And I say this again with no bullshit, folks. May God be with—"

We don't even get to hear him finish his sentence because the TV along with the rest of the power in the house goes out. The room is dim and yellow, lit only with the light of the setting sun.

Preppy gasps. "Shit, that was ominous as fuck. And he said bullshit on TV."

"You can say that again," King says with a sigh. He turns to Preppy. "Call Bear. I'll get started here. You know the drill."

"What drill?" I ask as Preppy pulls his phone from his pocket and races out the door.

"This ain't our first rodeo, pretty lady," Preppy replies in a southern cowboy style accent.

"Follow me," King says as he also pushes out the front door. I do as he says and follow him down the steps. Preppy peels out of the driveway as we reach King's shop which is attached to our garage. "We have a system in place. I put up the shutters and Preppy gathers the supplies. Food and medical. I'll call Bear and see if he plans on heading here or staying at the Clubhouse. Either way, he's in charge of water and generators."

"I've never been through a hurricane before," I admit.

"We've been through a few."

"How many like this?"

King shrugs. "Had a four once. The only difference is that it was predicted to come, and we were better prepared. Never had one that just changed directions like this before."

"A wild card hurricane. Unpredictable even when predictable."

"Preparation is the same for all of them. We just need to be a little faster when it comes to this one"

"But the reality of damage isn't. What about the addition and the kids—"

"Pup," King says, and I didn't realize he moved until he's right in front of me, cupping my face and forcing me to look up into his eyes. "All that matters is you, the baby in your belly, and the kids up in that house. The addition can fuck off. The house can fuck off. All the people of this town can fuck off. If we concentrate on what matters, we will be fine. I promise you that, and I would never fucking let anything happen to any of you. Ever."

"That's true when there are people coming after us, but you can't fight or shoot a hurricane."

King lifts the gun from the waistband of his jeans and smiles. "You wanna fucking bet?"

It turns out the gun is for after the storm in case looters came through and wanted to steal from homes they think are abandoned. The fact that anyone would take advantage of people like that, kicking them while they're down is disgusting, but just because I wouldn't do it doesn't mean it wasn't done and King was right.

We have to be prepared for anything and everything.

However, there are some things in life that no matter how much or little time you have, you'll never really be ready.

CHAPTER 5

RAY

"MOMMY, I'm worried about the hurricane," Max says, standing between my knees.

My heart aches that she's worried about something out of her control. "Hey, it's the adults' job to worry about those kinds of things. Stop trying to take my job, stinker."

"I'm not a stinker! Sammy's the stinker. Have you smelled his socks?"

"Unfortunately, I have," I say, tucking an unruly curl behind her little ear.

"Sammy, you're a stinker!" Max cries and runs back to chase her brother who is halfway up a tree.

King steps out onto the porch dressed in his usual all black with a plain black baseball cap on his head. "Hey, Pup." His voice is a deep bravado that tugs on every nerve-ending in my body. I thought it would fade over time, but it hasn't. Every day with him only amplifies my feelings.

Heart and body.

He sits on the step above me and looks out into the front yard where our kids are playing.

Nicole Grace is toddling around, chasing her brother and sister. Sammy and Max are shooting each other with massive water guns, gifts from Bear. I'm rocking the soon-to-be newest addition to our family in my protruding belly as I take in the laughs and squeals of delight coming from our ever-growing crazy brood.

"I've got to go meet with the guys and go over some shit. You good here for a while?" King asks.

"I'm good. Everything okay?" I ask.

"It will be," he responds, but I see worry in his eyes that wasn't there before. I'm about to ask him what's bothering him, besides the impending storm, but before I can get the question out of my mouth, we're interrupted by a small head of long blonde curls.

"Mommy! Daddy, remember when you got mawwied wifout us!" Max calls to us with her bottom lip stuck out in an adorable pout.

I smile at King. "The kids are still kind of pissed at us for getting married at the courthouse. They wanted to be there. They're more pissed about that than they were when I told them they can't play outside tomorrow because of the storm."

King gently places his hand on my throat. A possessive hold that I've come to love. "Yeah, but I couldn't wait any longer to marry you."

"Me, either," I admit.

He leans in and presses a soft kiss to my lips.

"Ewwwwwww!" Sammy cries.

We break apart and look to Sammy, who is pointing at us, wrinkling his little nose. "That's gross."

King laughs. "Mind your business, boy. You won't always think it's gross. Someday, you might even want to kiss a girl yourself."

Sammy shakes his head. "No way. It *is* gross, and I'm not changing my mind. Not now! Not ever!"

Max pops out from behind the thick trunk of the oak tree in the center of the yard and squirts Sammy from behind with her water gun. He lets out a shriek of surprise then takes off after her.

"Maybe, they need to see us get married," King suggests. "When all this shit is over."

My head snaps to him. "What?"

He watches the kids for a moment longer before turning to look at me. "I want them to see what's between us for what it is. Something good. Something strong." He stands and grabs my hand, pulling me up with him. His hand goes back to my throat and the other to my belly. "Go pick out a white dress, Pup. 'Cause after the sky clears and the baby is here, you and I are having ourselves a real wedding." He kisses me slowly, but it's not tender. It's a slow possession of my mouth and body. He pulls away, leaving me breathless. His eyes heavily lidded. "Now that you're mine in every way, I think that's something worth celebrating. Don't you?"

All I can do is nod because just like every time he kisses me, he's stolen my breath away.

"See you in a bit," he chuckles. "I've got to get some more screws for the shutters. I'll be back soon." He heads down the porch steps and runs up behind Sammy, lifting him up into the air so that Max can get a good shot at him. He puts down Sammy, and the kids take off running yet again.

King places a kiss on top of Nicole Grace's little icy-blonde head then walks over to his bike. Every stride he takes makes my breath quicken. He straddles the big black bike, and the engine roars to life. He flips his baseball cap around then takes off down the driveway.

I'm left gaping at him like a school kid with a crush because damn that man is still the most beautiful thing I've ever seen.

I go down into the yard and scoop up Nicole Grace, setting her on my hip. I yell to the other two kids that I'm going to put the younger one down for a nap.

When I emerge from the house a few moments later, Max and Sammy are sitting in the grass, watching ladybugs crawl over dandelions.

A car that I don't recognize pulls up on the driveway. My shoulders stiffen. My mind on full alert.

"Sammy, Max! Get inside, now!"

Sammy and Max do exactly as I order. Standing up and running past me into the house because they know my serious voice. They also know that mama doesn't play around when there's even a small possibility of a threat, especially when it comes to my kids.

I watch as a woman steps out from the shiny black BMW. She's beautiful and blonde. Thin with not a hair out of place. She's tall, wearing trendy large sunglasses and sky-high heels not meant for a gravel driveway, but somehow, she tackles the walk without a stumble.

"Is King around?" she asks, with a sweet southern drawl that makes my arm hairs stand on end. She glances up at the house and surrounding area before looking back up to me.

"Around here, we introduce ourselves before we ask questions," I tell her, crossing my arms over my chest.

She doesn't answer. Because she's distracted by something. She takes off her glasses and stares up into the front window where Max and Sammy are peering out over the top of the couch.

No, she's not looking at the kids as a whole. She's staring at Max.

Dread pools in my stomach as a thought crosses my mind and realization hits me like a bat to the chest.

No. It can't be.

She places her sunglasses atop her head. "As a matter of fact, there is something you can help me with," she says. "I don't know if King has told you about me, but I'm Tricia. I'm Max's—"

"You're not Max's fucking anything," I interrupt as blinding rage clouds my vision and makes my fists clench at my side.

She frowns, then straightens her shoulders as her lips flatten and her eyes grow wide with determination. "Oh, but, in fact, I am her *something*. A very significant *something* as it turns out. And by the looks of it, I think you know exactly who I am."

"*I'm* her mother. I have papers that will back that up and a gun that will back them up. So, why the fuck are you here?" I manage to grate out.

Tricia touches the tip of her sunglasses to the corner of her mouth. "Why, I'm here to see Max, of course. *My* baby girl."

Inside, I'm shaking. My heart is pounding. My protective nature kicks in, and I swear if I had a gun on me, I'd have leveled this woman on the gravel by now. Outside, I remain as cool and calm as I can.

I make my way slowly to the bottom step one slow step at a time until I'm eye to eye with the bitch. "You want to see my kid?" I chuckle because this will be the only warning I'm willing to give the bitch. "Over *your* dead body."

"We had a visitor," I tell King the second he pulls back up the driveway. My words tremble as they fall from my lips like grenades ready to explode at my feet. I feel my face pale. Speaking the words make what happened real, and it hits me that this woman could try and take my daughter from me.

"Who?" King asks, searching my eyes and gripping my shoulders.

I can't breathe. I can't fucking breathe. "Tricia. Max's..." I pause, not wanting to say the word *mom* as bile spins in my already upset stomach.

His fists curl around a piece of notebook paper in his hand, crushing it in his grip. "That would fucking explain this," King says, the veins in his forearms angrily protruding.

I unfold his fingers from the paper. "What is it?" I unravel what looks like a note.

King runs his hand through his hair and sucks in a deep breath. "Some fucking bullshit that was nailed to the garage door when I pulled up. A shipment was stolen from Pike and Nine a few days ago. A shipment I funded."

"Why didn't you tell me?"

"You've got a lot on your mind lately. I didn't want to worry you."

I want to be mad, but that would make me a hypocrite since I've been protecting King by keeping my troubles to myself as well.

King clears his throat. "I think it's safe to say that whoever is responsible for jacking the truck is the one who wrote this note. Too much of a coincidence with Tricia showing up like that. She likely brought it here herself."

I look down at the note.

King,

Your reign is over. There's a new King of the Causeway. I'll continue to make business in Logan's Beach impossible for you. I can take everything you have or you can hand it over. Give up your business in this town or give up the girl. The choice is yours.

Long live the King.

"I don't get it." I say, shaking my head. "Of course. The threat seems a little off."

"Yeah, I picked up on that too. Anyone who knows me knows that business means shit to me compared to family and I'd give it up easily. Whoever sent Tricia is using her as a pawn to so they can claim Logan's Beach as their own. I don't think their end game is Max. It's the money. Whoever it is, they've got a big fucking pair of balls crossing me like this."

I lift my eyes from the threat in my hand and look to King. "What are you going to do?"

"I'm going to start by telling everyone bringing business in or out of Logan's Beach to cease operations on whatever pays up to me. At least until we figure out who is behind this shit and slit the fucker's throat, we're at a standstill." He cups my face in his hands. "Don't worry. I can't and won't risk losing our daughter. I'll keep her safe. No matter the cost."

I turn the letter over in my hand as if there's more to read when the few words on the page say more than enough. "How are you going to find out who sent it?"

"My guess is that there's one person who knows." His eyes turn dark and cold. "And the second the storm passes, I'm going to find her."

Tricia.

"What if she won't tell you?" I ask, feeling stupid the second the words leave my mouth because I already know the answer before it leaves his lips.

"She will if she wants to keep breathing."

CHAPTER 6
RAY

I UNDERSTAND NOW why the phrase *the calm before the storm* is used. Because in the hours before Hurricane Polly brings her wrath upon Logan's Beach, everything is unusually still, including my usually racing heart which is frozen as it waits for what's to come.

The sky is clear of clouds. The breeze isn't gentle; it's nonexistent, as if holding its breath. Not a blade of grass is swaying. Not a bird is chirping. The bay waters don't dare to ripple.

Even the smell of salt and fish that usually lingers in the air is more salt and less fish. Like even they know that it's time to swim the fuck out.

Unfortunately, I don't think our unborn child received the same message.

The baby is coming. I feel it in the bones the same way I feel the shift in the air as the storm grows closer.

Please, just stay put a little while longer, little one. Just give me two days. Please. Not just because I'm a few weeks early, but because I don't want the baby born into chaos and that's exactly what life in our house and in our town looks like right now.

Pure and utter chaos.

The pains I've been feeling are still far apart and only as strong as a cramp, but they are growing more and more consistent with each hour that passes. The roads are closed. There will be no heading to a hospital anytime soon. *If only you can wait until you're scheduled c-section.*

If the new baby is as stubborn as it's father or myself, there's no amount of reasoning that's going to keep it inside of me if it's hell bent on entering the world.

"That's it. It's time to close this one, too." King says, placing the last remaining shutter over the window and climbing down the ladder. He folds it and stores it on a strap hooked to the wall in the open area under the house.

I follow him, but as soon as I take a step, I feel another pain. This one stronger than the others.

Stubborn. I knew it.

I press my hands over my belly and suck in a deep breath until the pain passes.

"Moving a lot?" King asks, pulling away and rubbing his hand over my stomach.

I nod and blink back my unshed tears. "We're fine. Just a little pain. It was the same way with Nicole Grace. Remember? There's no more room in there, so all of those pesky vital organs are getting in the way, not to mention my spine."

King holds me up even though the pain has passed, and I fold myself into his body, seeking support of a different kind. "That doctor is a fucking pussy," he mutters.

I smile against his chest. "Why?"

"Because, he's a fucking coward."

Now, I have to laugh. "He's a coward? Why, because he's out of town on his scheduled vacation three weeks before the baby is due?"

"That's part of it."

"And because he won't cater to your demand for him to find a flight that doesn't exist because the airport is shut down and fly back into ground zero of a hurricane zone where there's no power and the roads aren't passable so he can deliver our baby if and when we need him?"

"You sum it up better than I can."

"You're impossible."

"That might be true, but I'm still going to break every bone in that bastard's neck the next time I see him."

I pull back to swat at his chest. King catches my wrist and holds it against his chest. His eyes search mine, and I look away, uncomfortable under his determined gaze. Worried that he'll see everything I'm feeling inside because if he's sees it, then it will be real, and it's the last thing either of us need right now.

"Look at me, Pup."

I lift my chin, and reluctantly, my eyes meet his. "I'm here for you. You know that, right?" he asks into my hair. "You know that I've got you?" His words are about more than just the baby. There's a pain in his voice that packs a punch much stronger than the pains in my body.

I know he's here for me. That he's got me. I've always known that. I hate that he could think for one second that I doubt that. That I doubt him. It's others that I doubt. It's the storm that I doubt. It's my feelings that I doubt. It's every fucking thing else. But not King. Never King. "I know. And I'm behind you. All the way. Always."

King shakes his head and lifts my chin so my eyes meet his. "No, Pup, your place isn't *behind* me. It is, and has always been, *beside* me."

His words are a much-needed balm on my soul, and I can't help the feeling of both happiness and sadness that takes over. I don't know whether to kiss him or cry. It's like knocking over several colors of paint that pool together and end up in a brown mess. I can't discern one emotion from the other.

And I'm the fucking mess.

"Come with me." King takes my hand and leads me to the porch. For a while, we sit in silence with King rubbing my belly in a lazy circle.

"I love you," I tell him, placing my hand over his, feeling the words deep in my chest as they leave my lips. There is so much more in my words. So much I'm not saying, but I hope he feels the things I can't seem to be able to say.

"I love you." The sincerity in his eyes tells me he feels it.

I blink back my tears.

"Pup, you can talk to me. You know that. I know I ask this a lot, but are you okay? Because if you're not, it's fine and we can work through it. Together."

Are you okay? It's a question I've come to both loathe and love. A constant reminder that there is something wrong yet a reinforcement of how much he cares to keep asking.

There's so much I want to tell him. So much I want to try to explain, but I can't. I wouldn't even know where to start. But I'm done telling him that I'm fine or just tired. I can't lie to him anymore. It hurts too much, and he deserves more than lies, even if I'm not ready to explain the truth. I shake my head. "No, I'm not fine."

He raises his eyebrows, clearly, he was expecting one of those two aforementioned answers. "You can tell me anything. Talk to me about anything. I can take care of the shit with Trish and the shit with Nine's truck, but it's killing me that you won't even tell me what the problem is or that you say you're just tired when I know there's more."

How do I even begin to explain that in an attempt to not sink into the abyss growing in my brain I've been isolating myself. From my kids. From King. From life. Not physically, but emotionally. I've trapped myself in a panic room of my own making, terrified that if I open the door, my worst nightmares will be waiting for me on the other side. That over these past few months, I've frayed the chord that connects me with the ones I love. It's kept the worry at bay, but it's caused a different kind of pain that hasn't allowed me any rest or feel any true happiness.

"I think I need help. Actually, I know I do. Professional help," I admit, looking down at my hands. I'm surprised at the feeling of relief that comes with some of the weight being lifted from my body. It's a real physical feeling. Immediately, my shoulders straighten. The tightness in my chest is still there, but not nearly as constricting. I take a deep breath. My first in what seems like forever.

"Done," he says, pausing while waiting patiently for me to continue even though I know it's killing him because King doesn't do patience.

I sniffle and almost laugh at the absurdity of not being able to blurt out my problems to the man I love and person I trust most in this world. "I want to tell you more, and I will. I promise I'll tell you everything." I look up at the changing sky. "But if it's okay with you, I'd like to take this one storm at a time."

CHAPTER 7
RAY

"HOW ARE THEY DOING IN THERE?" King asks as I waddle from the hallway. He looks a lot less worried than before, and I'm relieved I could ease some of the tension with my confession and flatten the lines that have been an almost permanent fixture on his forehead.

"Nap time is in full swing. Preppy's reading NG a bedtime story. Or should I say a nap time story." I smile but it quickly turns to a cringe as another pain causes me to stop and hold onto the wall for support. This time, I'm panicking because again, it's stronger than the last one.

How long ago was the last one? An hour? Twenty minutes? I can't remember. Shit, I should be writing this down.

"Stay put in there," I whisper to the baby as the pain eases until it vanishes as if it was never here at all. "Please."

I didn't even notice King moved until he's standing right beside me, guiding me to the recliner. "You should be in a hospital," King mutters.

"Kind of hard between the roads being closed and that

whole bridge collapsing thing," I reply. "You've already called them a million times. Even if we could get there, they don't have any power, and their generators aren't working." Not only that, but the nurse who answered the phone told King that they're airlifting priority patients to another hospital until the wind gets too strong to keep the helicopter flying. I wouldn't be a priority patient. Most hospitals wouldn't even admit me at this stage. If this baby is going to come, we're on our own. "You're just mad they wouldn't send the helicopter to the house for me."

King grunts. "I know the flight medic. I'm gonna—"

"Break his neck?"

The side of his lip turns upward in a half smile. "I was going to say put a bullet in his head."

"Look at you, full of surprises," I tease.

He props a pillow behind my head. "Rest."

"I can't. I'm not even tired," I argue, but the second my head falls back into the softness now supporting my neck, I'm out.

I wake a little while later and find King asleep on the sofa next to me. His long legs propped over the armrest. The sight of his big body making the perfectly normal-sized sofa look like it belongs in a dollhouse makes me giggle just as another contraction hits. I hiss and count and breathe and do everything I can remember from movies when people go into labor. None of it works, but it does distract me until the pain passes.

Outside, a piece of wood flies by the window. The hurricane shutters King installed are clear. The rain passing by the window is horizontal. I admire it for a few seconds, then it suddenly shifts directions until it's spraying like a firehose against the shutter. The wind is loud. Much louder than I ever expected, almost like a car horn...if car horns could scream.

Hurricane Polly is here.

I push myself off the couch and check on the kids. They're all sleeping, safe and sound. Preppy is asleep on the floor of Nicole Grace's room with a bedtime story open on his lap. I shut the door softly, then waddle back into the living room and over to the window to get a better view of the storm. My worry over the hurricane is temporarily replaced by the fascinating goings-on outside. The rain shifts again, and then suddenly, it's gone, reduced to merely a drizzle, giving me a clearer view of what a hurricane really looks like.

Somewhere between the dirt and heaven, a kaleidoscope of grey and black clouds look like fingers, swirling wider and wider, intertwining in a supernatural handshake like jealous lovers preparing to rein down either revenge or redemption upon the Earth.

Darkness captures the sky like I've never seen before. Ominous. Thick. It's not even six p.m. yet the light fails to penetrate the clouds as if the sun's warmth and light never truly existed. A mere legend or myth. A god prayed to but never seen.

And then there's the rain.

Water gives life to all things. Plants. People. It cleanses and provides. Water is a good thing. No, a great thing.

Until it isn't.

Water as a single droplet is harmless. However, it grows more and more dangerous as the droplets join forces. I'm witnessing just that. Rain rushes to the earth like soldiers leaping from a plane. Once they land on the ground, they gather in units, forming various puddles around the yard and driveway, widening and rising until all the puddles merge together, forming a small river from one side of the yard to the other.

I pad over to the other side of the house. The backyard is under siege as well, but these soldiers aren't falling from the sky but crawling on their bellies from the bay, capturing more and more green space as it slowly descends upon the house.

"Shit," King mutters from behind me, observing the rising waters. "This is only the edge of the storm and the water's already rising."

"Do you think it will reach the house?"

"Probably, but that's why it's built on stilts, so the flood waters can't reach us."

"Where's Bear and Thia in all this?" I ask.

"Bear's at the club. With the new renovations, it will hold. If the water rises to the first floor we'll head up to the bonus room on the second."

If there was doubt before, there isn't now. We are in the middle of the biggest disaster of our lives.

And also, the hurricane is here.

"Mom?" Sammy asks, emerging from his bedroom, rubbing his sleepy eyes with his fists. "Where is Maxie?" Sammy asks, rubbing his sleepy eyes with his fists.

My entire body freezes, trapped in an iceberg of fear. King and I exchange a quick glance, and without hesitation, he darts down the hall. He comes back, looking tousled and frantic. His bright green eyes as wild as I'm sure mine are.

"She's not in there," he says, running through the kitchen. He checks every cabinet. Then the pantry.

"Nicole Grace?" I ask.

"Sleeping," he replies.

I tug on Sammy's hand and lower myself to his eye level. "Where did Maxie go, sweetie? Did you see?" I'm unable to hide the tremble in my voice.

He shakes his head.

King slowly raises his eyes to mine and answers the question the second they lock without saying a word. *She didn't go anywhere. She was taken.*

"No!" I want to cry, but I don't want to scare Sammy.

The screen door at the back of the house flaps in the wind, and King wastes no time running in that direction. I raise myself to my feet, and it takes forever because my mind is already at the back door with King.

"I don't know where she went. I woke up, and she was gone," Sammy says, following close behind.

King looks out the door in both directions. "Nothing. The door was open, but the screen door was shut. I'll go check the garage and the treehouse. Maybe, it's not what we think, and she's just hiding."

"I'll go with you," Preppy says.

King and Preppy run out into the rain which chooses that moment to open up onto the earth like the ocean is falling from the sky. If Max is out there in this...*no*. I won't let my thoughts go there.

She'll be fine. She has to be fine.

Sammy tugs on the sleeve of my sweater. "Will Maxie be okay?"

I brush his soft hair back on his head. "She'll be fine.

Daddy's going to get her now. Why don't you go sleep in Mommy and Daddy's bed for a little while?"

He nods and pads sleepily down the hall, content with his mommy's assurance that Max will be okay.

I really hoped what I told him wasn't a lie.

Another contraction hits, and this time, I don't breathe through it. Instead, I grit my teeth and wait for it to pass. When it does, I realize I can't just stand there, so I recheck every possible hiding space in the house for Max but come up empty.

Another contraction hits me, and it's so strong that when it passes, I find myself on my knees in the middle of the kitchen.

"Mommy!" I hear a small voice in the distance, and at first, I think it's my imagination or the wind.

"Mommy!" It's not the weather or my brain calling to me.

It's my daughter.

Max's cries are an adrenaline shot straight to my heart. I hope that King heard her, too, but I can't rely on it. I have to get to her. It's my only thought. My only purpose.

I head for the front door toward the sound of her cries. On instinct, I reach into the side table drawer and grab the handgun King keeps there. It's on a belt, so I throw it over my shoulder.

What greets me outside is the storm beginning to flex its muscles.

Twisted metal, what looks like used to be the poles that held up the *Welcome to Logan's Beach* sign, crashes into the house, but I can't hear the impact over the wind howling in my ear like a wolf cry in the night.

The metal piece crashes against the house again and again, turning and flopping like a fish out of water. It scrapes along the roof, tearing off shingles, before launching over the back of the house.

I duck to avoid one of the rectangular-shaped shrapnel pieces spinning in my direction. I barely manage to avoid decapitation when another hits me hard, landing flat against my back with blunt force that rips the air from my lungs. I stagger forward, trying to maintain my balance. The wind makes it hard to fill my lungs again, and it seems like forever until I'm able to take a breath that is actually productive.

I trudge forward in the shin-deep brown water. Each step meets resistance and feels as if there's a hundred-pound weight strapped to each of my thighs. I shield my eyes from the stinging rain and try to blink away the water blurring my vision as I search the water for any sign of Max.

A contraction hits me so hard I temporarily go blind. The pain can come. I don't give a shit about pain right now. I do need my sight to find Max however and the number of seconds it takes me to regain the use of my eyes seems like an eternity.

I'm halfway through the front yard when I see Tricia shoving Max into the backseat of her car. The water is halfway up her tire. Most of the roads are closed. There's literally shrapnel flying around in every direction. The pain and anger I feel surging through my veins over her trying to take my daughter overwhelms me, but coming in a close second is the fact that this bitch's plan is a shitty one and she's putting Max in danger in order to carry it out.

Max spots me. "Mommy!"

Tricia turns and sees me coming and tries again to push Max through the door, but my girl won't budge, kicking her legs out to avoid being pressed inside. "I'm your mommy now," Tricia says through her teeth.

I pull King's gun and aim it at her head and cock it.

"You're really going to kill me for taking back my own daughter?" she says with an evil laugh and a roll of her eyes. She's got her arms around Max as she turns to face me, using her as a shield against a potential bullet.

I see fucking RED. Rivers of red. Motherfucking oceans of red.

"She's not yours. Never was. You lost that chance. And if you wanted to visit her, there are other ways than to take her during a fucking hurricane from her rightful parents," I say with every ounce of anger I feel flowing through me. "Let her go, or I'll blow your fucking head off."

Max's eyes are trained on mine and less frightful than they were when Tricia was trying to shove her into the car. Because I'm her mom. Because she knows I'll make it all okay. Because she trusts me.

I will not let you down, I say to Max with a silent look.

"Such language around the child," Tricia says, pulling Max closer to her and then lifting her up into her arms. Max struggles against her, but she holds her tighter. "Shoot me, and you risk shooting her," she says triumphantly.

"Why?" I ask, lowering my weapon so it's not aimed at my child. "Just tell me, why are you doing this? It doesn't make sense. After all this time."

Tricia's smile fades. "He...he wants children. He won't marry me because I can't have any more." Her smile returns, and she jostles Max in her arms. "But I'm going to bring him my child, *our* child. He said we can be a family, and we'll get married, and everything will be okay." She looks to Max whose big eyes are still trained on me. Her voice is softer when she repeats, "Everything will be okay," she says as if she's trying to convince herself of her own lie.

"Even if you could get her in that car, the water has risen to the top of your tire. You can't drive her out of here. The roads are closed and flooded. The bridge is down."

"There's always a way. Mothers always find a way when it comes to their children."

Yes. Yes, they do. At least, that we can agree on.

"So, this is your idea of motherhood? Taking her from her loving home so she can be payment for the life you want for yourself? By risking her life in a storm so you can live out some distorted leave it to beaver dream?" I shout as rain pelts me from all sides while I look for my next move. I have to get to Max without risking her getting hurt, but I'll have to wait for an opening. A movement. Anything.

"My idea of motherhood is being a mother to *my* daughter," she replies.

The water is continuing to rise. I can see Tricia struggling to stay on her feet as it rushes by her.

"No, you've got it all wrong. Being a mother is about the crazy shit that you'd do for yourself it's about the crazy shit you'd do for your kids. Besides, whoever this mystery guy is, he's using you to get what he wants. Think about it. He knows King would do anything for his kids, including giving up control over Logan's Beach. It was in the demand letter you delivered yourself. You were never going to have her because it's not what he really wanted. He wanted the money. He's been playing you this entire time, making you believe it's about family when it's only ever been about one thing. Greed."

Tricia is about to reply when a surge of water like a wave in the ocean washes over them. Max screams as the water sweeps her out of Tricia's arms, and they are both lost to the current.

"No!" I scream, choking on the rain in my throat.

Without thinking about anything but Max, I rush forward and dive in, letting the rushing water carry me toward my daughter.

Because fuck it.

Fuck this life.

I'll gladly give mine for hers. Right here. Right now.

Not just gladly. Enthusiastically.

Because as long as she lives, and she will live, my life is a small trinket to trade in exchange for such a return.

I try to float above the water but every so often my foot catches on something that pulls me under. When I emerge, I've lost sight of Max, until I hear her scream again. I glance in the direction of her voice and see her hanging onto a piece of wood that looks like the top of her swing set. I don't fight the water. There's no point. It's too fast. Too strong. Instead, I make myself as wide as I can, spreading my arms and legs in hopes that it will hook onto the playset. If I can just get close enough. I calm my breathing even as my daughter's screams grow louder, and my every instinct is calling on me to try and swim to her.

Another wave takes me under, but when I emerge again, I see the playset. I'm almost on it. Max is still clinging to the pole, but she cries out as she begins to slip.

I let out a raw scream as I reach my limbs as far as they can go. I manage to hook my foot around the wood under the water connecting to the piece Max is clinging to. Pain slices through me, either another contraction or something in the water slicing me, but I don't have time to be in pain. I pull myself up on the wood and reach for Max's hand.

"Reach for me!" I yell to her over the wind and rain.

She leans out and extends her shaking little hand. I grab it and pull her to me, setting her against my huge belly. "Hey, there. Fancy seeing you here," I say, relieved at the weight of her in my arms, a feeling that for a moment I didn't know if I'd ever experience again. Even with rain and tears streaming down my face, she manages to smile at my joke.

"You have to hold on tight, baby. Can you do that for me? Just for a few more minutes?"

She nods and grips the wood as tight as she can. We only have another minute or two before we are completely submerged once again, so I have to think fast. I guide myself, one hand over the other along the top of the swing set until my hand finds the metal chain connecting the swing. I unhook both chains and tie one end around my waist. I'm going to tie this around your waist okay?"

She nods as I tie her to me. I take both swings and push them between the chains and our bodies to act as floats. Hopefully, it will keep us above water so we can be found.

I don't have time to contemplate it before we're swept up in the water yet again. We manage to stay upright as I float on my back with my daughter on my chest above my stomach, but I don't know how long I'll be able to hold this position. Floating debris collides with my shoulder, and I know I'm bleeding, but fuck blood. Blood doesn't matter. It never did.

It never would.

Not in our family.

"Are you okay?" I call out to Max.

"I'm scared, Mommy," she replies.

"Don't be. Mommy's got you. Mommy wouldn't ever let anything happen to you. You know that, right?"

She nods against my neck.

"Good. I've got you. I've always got you."

I look around for something to grab, but I don't see anything but water and the tops of some trees.

The sound of the rushing water grows louder and louder until I realize it's not the water at all.

Two wave runners emerge from the back of the house and speed toward us, racing ahead of us. They stop just before the billboard, and just before we crash into it, we're lifted from the water by out of this world strong arms and placed over King's lap. "Maxie, are you okay, baby?" he shouts over the wind.

"Yes, Daddy. Mommy saved me."

He looks over at me. "I know. She saved me, too, baby. She saved me, too."

King hits the throttle and heads back to the house. The water is so high now it covers the first floor. King kills the engine and pulls alongside a window to the bonus room on the second floor. The window opens. We stop below an open window, and King unchains Max from me, hoisting her up to Bear's waiting arms. King turns me so that my belly faces away from the house and lifts me by my thighs, not letting go until Bear has me seated on the window ledge. Carefully spinning me back around, he cradles me in his arms, then sets my feet on the floor, but my legs give out, and I fall to my knees.

"Hello there, darlin'," Bear drawls as if we just ran into each other at the local bar.

Max rushes into my arms. "Mommy!"

"Oh, Maxie. My brave girl." I hold her as tight as I can while tears stream down my already wet cheeks.

Bear tosses a warm blanket over our shoulders just as a bang sounds against the wall. King's hands appear on the ledge. Bear gives him a hand and helps him inside.

King rushes to us, wrapping us both in his arms. "I was so afraid I was going to lose you," King says, his voice frantic. "So fucking afraid. Tricia wasn't alone. She had guys waiting for us by the garage. They shot at us. We took two of them down before I could get to you. I was so fucking afraid."

"I'm fine. We both are," I assure him, relieved to be able to speak the words out loud.

"I can't believe you did that. You went out there," he says, searching both myself and Max for any visible injuries.

"I had to," I say, "I had no choice. The door was open. I heard her calling for me." My chest tightens as I replay the events in my head. "I had to," I repeat.

King presses his forehead to mine. He grips the back of my neck and holds me to him as close as he can. "I know, baby. I fucking know," his voice cracks.

Sammy bursts into the room and crashes his way into the family hug. For a few moments, we say nothing.

Thia comes into the room holding Nicole Grace.

"When did you guys get here?" I ask, finally able to catch my breath.

Thia frowns. "The house is underwater, and the club's roof is gone. We took the boat and made it here just before the water rushed in."

"I'm glad you're all okay," I say.

Thia smiles and looks at our family. Sopping wet in a pile on the floor. "Ditto."

"Can I say a potty word mommy?" Maxie asks, tugging on my wet shirt.

I smile into her hair. "Sure, why not? Potty words seem a little silly after what we just went through, but just this once."

She stares up at me, cupping her mouth with her hand, I bend as far as my big belly will allow to hear her better. "That lady is a real pee pee head," she whispers.

King chuckles. Apparently, Preppy and I aren't the only ones who need to work on our whispering skills.

I kiss her on the top of her wet curls. "Yeah, she is. She most definitely is."

"Was," King says, so only I can hear.

"Was what?" I ask.

"She *was* a pee pee head."

I raise an eyebrow. "And what is she now?"

A soaking wet Preppy walks into the room, straightening his soggy bow-tie. "Dead."

Max and Sammy wriggled free from our hold and are now playing with Bear's kids in the corner of the room. Nicole Grace is asleep in Thia's arms.

Preppy and King saw Tricia's body floating face-first by the shed, and I can't help but feel bad for her. She may not have really wanted to be a mother, but she did want to be loved, and she was willing to sacrifice anything or anyone to get it.

My stomach tightens, and I feel like I'm being ripped apart from the inside out. "Ahhhhh!"

King moves closer to my side and asks a silent question, concern and worry lining his face once again.

I nod because I can't answer him. The pain is too great.

And just as it ebbs, it starts a new. I feel a pressure like I've never felt before, and there's no doubt about what's happening.

King tells Thia to take the kids into the bedroom attached to the bonus room. Preppy appears with some blankets.

King puts his arms around my shoulders to lift me, but I shake my head. "There's no time," I manage to say as my entire body contorts from the pain as if I'm possessed by a demon.

I tap my hand against the maternity leggings, and King moves to swiftly to peel the wet pants and underwear down my legs.

"What do you need me to do?" King asks.

"Ahhhhhhhhh..." I scream as the pain hits me harder than any other wave before it. This time, I give in to the need to push and bare down as hard as I can until I feel a blood vessel pop in my eye. There's this burning, tearing feeling between my legs, and it's like being sliced and set on fire at the same time.

King looks down. "I see the head. You've got this, baby. You're the strongest person I know. You've got this." I focus on King's eyes as another contraction sits on my stomach like an anvil. The pain is greater than I knew was possible, but even as it wreaks havoc on my body, my instinct kicks in, and as I push one more time and my vision turns to static, I reach down and feel for my baby.

King raises up on his knees and watches with both fear and wonderment as I deliver our new baby into the world. I pull her from my body and set her on my chest. King wipes her with a clean sheet, and although she's not crying, I know she's okay because bright blue eyes stare up at me in wonderment.

The pain is gone as if it never was.

King covers us both in a blanket, and I look up at my

husband.

"Holy fucking shit," Preppy says from the corner of the room. "Are you a fucking superhero or something because I feel like you should have told me a while ago, and frankly, I'm a little butt hurt about it."

"Fuck yeah, she is," King says, with pride in his voice that surges into my chest. He covers me and our new baby with another soft, clean blanket. "I can't believe she's here. I can't believe what you just did."

Preppy clears his throat. "Uh, is this a good time to let you know that what I just saw down there was a fucking shit show, but for some reason, I've got a chubby." He scratches his beard. "And for the first time in my life, even I'm concerned about my mental status."

"Prep," King warns.

"I'll give you two some space," Preppy says, as if his leaving was voluntary and not because King is demanding it with his eyes. He heads toward the door. "I hope the cell service is back up soon. I gotta talk this through with Doc." I can still hear him muttering to himself on the other side of the door. "Maybe, I should start going to church…"

I look down at our newest little one whose wrapped her little hand around my index finger. She makes a noise like an amused grunt, and I chuckle. "I have the perfect name for her."

King smiles knowingly. "I think I can guess what it is."

I press a kiss on the top of our daughter's tiny head. "Welcome to the world, Polly Storm King."

We may have named her after a hurricane, but she'll be no match for one.

I rest my head against King's chest.

Just like her parents.

CHAPTER 8

RAY

SIX WEEKS LATER...

The generator powering our refrigerator and lights, the one on our porch that's been running twenty-four hours a day for the past six weeks, is louder than a lawnmower, but after six weeks, I'm used to it. The vibration in my ear drums has become the new normal.

Polly is propped on the counter in her bouncy seat while I heat her bottle. I check the temperature of her formula on my wrist. It's perfect. "Alright, baby girl. Lunch is served." I look down only to find that Polly is now fast asleep.

I smile and set the bottle down. "I guess lunch will have to wait," I whisper, running the back of my index finger over her plump little cheek. I carefully unbuckle her from the seat and carry her into our bedroom where I place her in her bassinet and adjust her soft swaddling blanket.

I check my phone to make sure the baby monitor is working before heading out into the living room.

"Ray?" A voice asks. Preppy's wife Dre pops her head

through the open screen door. "Sorry, I didn't want to just come right in. I rang the bell, but this damn thing is so loud out here I didn't know if you heard it or not."

I hadn't. "Come on in," I say. "How was New York?"

Dre smiles and steps inside. "Thanks. It was great, but if I'm being honest, I love my father, but these past few weeks have been the longest of my life. We took the first flight back after the airport reopened."

I return her smile. I'm happy to see my friend again.

I pause and my smile grows wider.

Happy.

I've felt a lot better over these past few weeks, but this is the first time, I've been able to place that word with something I was feeling.

"What's got you all smiley?" Dre asks, taking a seat at the breakfast bar.

I shake my head. "Just happy to see you."

"That makes two of us."

"Preppy and King are outback with the brood." I round the counter into the kitchen and grab a mug from the cabinet. "Coffee? Tea? Beer?" I ask Dre.

She flattens her hands on the counter. "Nope. They aren't. Preppy and Bear took the whole lot of them to Bear's house to check out the new playground Thia built, and the only thing I want right now is to keep watch over that baby of yours while you go take some me time."

I put the mug away. "That's okay. You don't have to—"

"I know I don't, but I'm doing it anyway, and I'm not taking no for an answer. Where is the little miracle?"

"She's sleeping in her bassinet in our room," I say slowly.

Dre claps her hands together. "Great."

"The bottles are—"

"Not my first rodeo, Ray!" She calls out to me, already halfway down the hall.

"You're starting to sound a lot like your husband, you know," I call back.

She looks over her shoulder. "I mean it. Go take some time for yourself, and don't come back because I'll just send you back out again." She winks and carefully opens the bedroom door, disappearing inside and shutting it quietly without so much as a click.

I look around the quiet living room.

Now, what the fuck am I supposed to do?

I shove my feet into my flip flops and head outside. The sunlight is warm against my skin. The generator is deafening but thankfully fades as I pass it on my way to cut through the backyard to the bay.

The scent of salt and fish is as it was before the storm, lightly perfuming the humid air.

I walk past the addition and stop to look it over. It was severely damaged during the storm. What was left of the framing had to be torn down and rebuilt. But King's enlisted the help of a contractor, and after repairing our damaged roof and the flood-damaged siding of the existing house, they made quick work of getting back to the business of expanding the house. Now, it looks like part of the house, an unpainted part, but part nonetheless. I run my fingers across the grey stucco and feel the excitement of using all the new space being created.

I don't dare go inside. King has already warned me that I'm not to go in until it's complete because it's not safe.

My thoughts turn to the storm and how I was able to save Max while pregnant, while in labor, during a hurricane.

And King's worried about me stepping on a nail or something.

I chuckle at the thought.

The wet air feels sticky and warm against my pale skin as I head through the grass toward the water, which is now back in its proper place within the bay. I sit and dangle my feet over the edge. The setting sun glistens off the water, and this far from the angry noise of the generator, I can actually hear the birds rustling the trees and occasional splash of a jumping mullet.

I close my eyes and lean back in the grass, but the second my eyes are shut, I realize that something's missing from me entirely enjoying the moment.

Someone.

The man who has been everything to me for years. Suddenly, I feel guilty for how he must have been feeling while I was trapped under the haze for not being myself. King's still every much the man I fell in love with all those years ago, but who am I now?

He must have heard my thoughts because, suddenly, I hear his deep voice above me, rumbling into my skin and covering me with more warmth than the sun ever could.

"Tell me what you're thinking," he says.

I open my eyes, and his beautiful face comes into view. Bright green eyes peer down at me with concern and love. I pat the concrete space next to me, and King sits, our thighs touching.

We haven't talked much since the hurricane. In all honesty, there hasn't been time. And with everything that happened during the hurricane, I think both of us were content with just knowing that everyone was alive and safe and the conversation, seeming much less important in the face of death, was temporarily put on a shelf.

It's time.

"I was just thinking that I'm not the same innocent girl I was when we met," I admit.

King points to the tattoo on my back. The one he gave me years before. He runs the pads of his fingers over the words written into the elaborate vine design. *I don't want to repeat my innocence. I want the pleasure of losing it all over again.*

"You're right. You're not," King says.

I'd be lying if I didn't say I felt a twinge of hurt at his words.

He continues, "When we met, I thought you were the sexiest fucking thing I'd ever saw. You were feisty and quick-witted, and the way you defied me made me want you even more. After we got together, I didn't think it was even possible for you to grow even smarter or sexier than you already were." His voice deepens. "Or make me harder than you did, but you do. Yeah, you've changed. Because you're more now. Not less. Not entirely different, but *more*."

I remain silent because his words have stilled my tongue and stirred every other emotion. Ones that aren't pooling in a puddle of brown, but separate and identifiable.

King leans back in the grass, keeping himself propped up on his hands. "You've lived. You've grown. It happens to everyone. Even me."

I can't help but ask, "What about Preppy?"

He quirks an eyebrow, the one with the scar through the middle. "Good point. Okay, maybe that doesn't apply to Preppy." He laughs at his own joke. The sound wraps around me. Deep and pure it invades my senses, and even after all these years I still feel his laugh vibrating throughout my entire body, vibrating straight through to my heart. "Does it bother you? That you've changed?"

"No, but I keep thinking that I'm not her anymore. The girl you fell in love with." My cheeks burn with the admission. He may be forcing me to face him but my eyes lock on a patch of grass between us.

"Look at me," he demands.

I want to look at him, but I'm still too embarrassed.

"Pup, look at me," he repeats.

I finally raise my eyes to meet his. They're beautiful and bright under the full moon, but there's anger in them that hadn't been there a few moments ago. The space between his brows lined with a deep frown. "The younger versions of ourselves are not the better versions." His hand seeks finds mine and large fingers thread through my small ones. Tanned skin on pale, resting on my upper thigh. "Don't you see that? You're so much more now. So much fucking more."

His bright green eyes appear even brighter under the glow of the full moon. "Do you remember when I told you that you scared the shit out of me?"

I recall the memory and the words we exchanged that night inside of his truck while we watched Max from a distance.

"I've been in a maximum-security prison. I've been around the worst of the worst. I've had to sleep with one eye open, thinking my next breath could be my last," King says.

"Why are you telling me all this?" I ask.

He turns toward me and our eyes lock. He reaches out and

runs the back of his pointer finger along my cheek. "Because I want you to know that none of those motherfuckers ever scared me as much as you do."

My body warms at the memory. I graze my fingertips against my cheek as if I can still feel the warmth of his touch from that night. "I do remember."

How could I ever forget?

"Pup, I was scared of that innocent version of you," King's lips remain flat as he looks back over the bay. He covers our joined hands with his other hand. He turns at the waist, his upper half now facing me. He reaches out and cups my face in both of his hands. "Now, you're a mother who would do anything to protect her kids at any cost."

"So, you're not scared of me anymore." It's not a question. I hate the sound of defeat in my voice and how deflated I feel inside.

"No, Pup, you don't get it." King growls. His gaze bores into mine. "I was scared of you back then. Now?...I'm fucking terrified."

King was never great at words, and so he drives his point home, communicating the way he knows will get his point across.

His lips claim mine in a raw, emotional possession of my mouth and my soul.

He pulls back, leaving me wanting more and hating the space between us, so I fill the space with long overdue words. I take a moment to collect my thoughts and wipe my sweaty palms on my jeans. I take a deep breath because King's right. It's time to tell him everything.

"Since Nicole Grace was born, it's been like there's this... this thing. This entity of hopelessness weaving its way inside my body, like a parasite, telling me that it's impossible for me to be happy. Like at any second, all of this could go away. You. The kids. I can't lose any of you. I was walking around feeling nothing but worry or guilt every single second of the day and most of the night because I couldn't sleep. You, the kids, you're everything to me. The thought that anything could happen to any of you at any time was overwhelming me, making the smallest tasks seem like climbing a mountain. I shut down. And then with the hurricane coming and then Tricia showing up...it all just exacerbated those feelings. It became too much. The voice inside my head grew louder and the hopelessness dug its nails into me even deeper."

"I'm sorry you went through that." King says, reaching for my hand. "How do you feel now?"

I smile. "I was just thinking about that when Dre came over. "Happy. For the first time in a long time, I feel happy."

King's eyes brighten. "Good. So fucking good." He presses a kiss to my head, and I hear the relief in his words. He sighs into my hair, and it's like I can feel some of the worry leaving him with his breath.

"You know, when I was out there in the hurricane trying to get to Max and I was terrified, but then I remembered something someone very important once told me. Something I'd forgotten in the haze," I say, looking up into his eyes.

"What was it?"

I squeeze his hand. "Stop being alive, and start living. Your words. It was your voice pushing me on when the other voice was trying to pull me down. Somewhere in between the time I jumped in the water and the time I reached Max, I realized that things happen. Hurricanes happen. Tragedies happen. I made a promise to myself that when it was all over and Max was safe that I would fight against the voice and do everything I could in order to not spend my time worrying about when the other shoe is going to drop. I have to live instead of being afraid of the things life could bring." I sigh. "I mean, it was easier said than done. It wasn't like I magically thought I would be better and poof it happened. The fading hormones and antidepressants have played a big part in that."

The day after I gave birth, the roads were cleared and King was able to take me and Polly to the hospital to make sure there were no post-birth complications. That's when I met Ruby, the nurse who listened to me as I cried and broke down and told my life story. She's also the one who pulled a doctor into my room from the hallway and forced him to write me a prescription for antidepressants right then and there.

I look to King who doesn't appear as surprised as I thought he would be.

He smiles at my confused expression. "Pup, I know. I talked to the nurse at the hospital. She told me everything. Well, I made her tell me everything. Told her I would show up every day if she didn't."

"You did?" I raise my eyebrows. I shouldn't be surprised

"Of course, I fucking did. Why do you think I've been giving you so much space? Why I haven't been asking you if you're okay? She told me not to and that you'd talk when you're ready and I shouldn't push you."

"And you listened?"

"It wasn't fucking easy," he admits. "But you're so brave. Admitting you needed help and getting it. My only problem was admitting that I can't always be the one who will be able to help you, and that just don't sit right with me. But I realized that I could help you, by sending Ruby to your room."

"You know Ruby? That traitor."

"I know everyone in this town, Pup. You should know this by now. I was locked up with her brother. She used to sneak us in these little turkey pot pies." He lifts my hand to his mouth and kisses my fingers. "I don't know what she said to you, but I'm glad she helped you."

I trace my fingers over the scar lining his eyebrow. "Me, too. She said what I have is long-term postpartum depression, exasperated by pregnancy hormones. I always thought that postpartum was something that went away after you had a baby, but she said it's different in all women and can sometimes last for years. They may need to tweak them as time goes on but right now, I feel...a lot better. And when Ruby told me her own story of how she went through the same thing, I felt, I don't know, less alone."

"Pup, you're never in this alone."

The cringe of guilt rears its ugly head. "I wanted to tell you. I did. I tried to, several times. But I didn't understand what was going on myself, and the thought of coming to tell you that I feel sad or off felt silly and selfish."

"Selfish is the furthest thing you could ever be. And there's nothing you can't tell me, but I understand why you didn't. I don't like it, but I understand it." He presses his forehead against mine, and I inhale the smell of soap and the faint trace of cigarettes. "Make me a promise. In the future when you ain't feeling right, even if you can't explain it or understand why, just tell me something's not right. I won't try, and fix it. I'll just be here for you. I am here for you. Always."

"When did you become so wise?" I ask with a sniffle as my chest swells and the love I feel for King spills from my eye.

King wipes the tear with his thumb and sucks it into his mouth. "When Preppy rose from the dead."

I scrunch my nose. "Huh?"

He chuckles. "Nothing, I'll explain it to you later. Better, yet, I'll let Preppy ramble on about it."

"There is one more thing I have to tell you," I admit, biting my lower lip.

"Tell me anything," he says.

I lick my bottom lip and watch as King's eyes follow the movements of my tongue. "When I went for my follow up appointment today, the doctor gave me another prescription. One you don't know about."

He stills. "For what?"

I put my arms around his neck and pull him closer. "For you. It's been six weeks."

Kings eyes darken, his lids hooded. "Now that's one I can help you fill."

The anticipation heats the air between us. King stands and lifts me into his arms.

"You don't have to carry me!" I squeal.

His voice is low and dark, full of raw desire and emotion. "I carried you back then. I carry you now. I'll carry you. Always."

CHAPTER 9

RAY

THERE HAVE BEEN SO many moments when I've not felt good enough or strong enough over the past few months, but being with King, like this, is a reminder of clarity. Of what matters.

Of us.

King kisses me passionately, a slow burn that builds into an inferno with one swipe of his tongue against mine. When he pulls back, it's only so he can navigate the stairs, taking two at a time until we're alone in the new addition of the house. It's dark and empty, but I see more clearly than ever before.

I see King.

I'm nervous, although I know I shouldn't be. It's been a while, but there's no doubt what I want, and what I want is him. All of him. Forever.

Now.

"I ache for you, Pup. Now, more than ever." He stalks over to me. The muscles of his strong thighs flexing beneath his tight jeans. "Did you know that? Do you know what you fucking do to me?"

I shake my head. My legs tremble.

"Well, now, you do," he says. He's standing right in front of me, not touching me. "What do you want, Pup?"

I don't hesitate, my words come out breathless. "You. I want you."

He groans and wraps his large hand around my throat, firm and strong. A possessive warning of what's to come.

My body shudders, and my pulse quickens.

King walks me backward until I collide with the wall. "Is this what you want, Pup?" His other hand rises on my outer thigh, lighting a fire on my skin. He pushes up my dress, exposing my damp panties.

"Yes," I breathe.

King lifts me from the wall and turns me around, pulling me down on the floor, and I fall gracelessly onto the carpet.

Desire is the yearning to erase all distance. That's exactly what I want. To erase the distance between myself and King. Both the distance in my head and the three feet or so between us right now.

He hovers over me and pops the button on my shorts, slowly unzipping them. I lift my hips eagerly.

King shakes his head. "Patience, Pup. I'm taking my time with you tonight." He pulls my shorts down my legs, and he wasn't kidding. He is taking his time. His fingers drag against the bare skin of my thighs, and I'm awash in sensation and need that's sending blood racing through my ears like heavy rain on pavement.

He tosses my shorts to the floor and grabs my knees, spreading my legs wide to accommodate his large body between them. He licks me over my panties, and I convulse at the contact.

He chuckles low in his throat, and I arch my back. Why isn't he in more of a rush? *I don't know how much of this I can take*, I think as he makes another swipe at my clit with his talented tongue.

He removes my panties, and now, I'm left only in his shirt, naked from the waist down.

If the sensation of his tongue against my panties made me jump, the feeling of it against my clit with no barrier between makes me practically leap off the bed with every muscle and nerve in my body reacting to the shock of pleasure I'm now feeling everywhere.

"I've missed this beautiful pussy," he growls, lightly scraping his teeth over my inner thigh. For a moment, he lingers there, just staring. I try to close my thighs, thinking something is wrong or that it doesn't look the way it used to, but his head is in the way, and all I manage to do is clamp my legs around his ears.

He pushes my knees wide once more and holds me there. "Pup," he warns. King flattens his tongue and licks me from ass to clit, sucking on it lightly before releasing it. "I've waited a long, fucking time to see this beautiful body of yours again, and I plan on spending my sweet time appreciating every fucking part of you and getting reacquainted. You're the sexiest fucking thing I've ever seen, and so is every part of you." He rises to his knees and takes my hand, guiding it to where his erection is straining behind his jeans. "I've never been so damn hard in my life. It's all for you. Always for you."

I gasp. I know it's been a while, but somehow, he seems even larger than he had before.

He lowers himself back down over my body. "No more hiding from me," he says. "Not now. Not ever. Are we clear?"

I nod because I can't find the words. Not just because he's hooked a finger inside of me while circling my clit with his tongue but because I don't know what to say that can make him understand how much his words mean to me. I know he loves me. I know I'm beautiful. I know what amazing things my body has created and been through. I've known all along. I just haven't been able to connect my brain and my heart and get them on the same page, but that's exactly what King is doing. Connecting the two once more.

And for the first time in a while, I believe him. I feel beautiful. I feel wanted. And I WANT.

Oh, fuck, do I want.

King growls into my pussy as I feel a flush of wetness release with my increased desire. "That's it, Pup. You're so fucking wet for me. So fucking ready."

"So take me," I pant. "Now."

He shakes his head. The stubble on his face adding a new feeling of sensation, adding to the growing ache in my body. "Not yet. Not until you come."

He inserts another finger, and my eyes roll back in my head as he pulls out and pushes back in with a rhythm that has me riding both his fingers and his face as he relentlessly sucks, licks, nips at my clit and the outer folds. He removes his fingers and lightly pinches the outer folds of my pussy together, putting pressure on my clit. He massages them together with my poor sensitive clit within then covers it with his mouth, and my head falls back on the pillow. My back arches, and he pushes his tongue right into the spot I need it one last time.

I swear I go fucking blind from the pleasure of it all. From him.

I'm not in the room anymore or on the floor. I'm on another planet where I'm floating above myself, watching the sexiest scene I've ever laid eyes on unfold beneath me. King between my legs. King bringing me pleasure. King making me come until I'm sure I'm blacking out.

When I come to, King is between my legs with the thick head of his hot throbbing erection prodding at the entrance to my soaking, wet pussy. He grabs his shaft and rubs the head through my wetness, and I groan, the need building even faster this time. My lower stomach is tight and so is every nerve ending working overtime to hold my body together and keep it from exploding from sheer fucking pleasure.

"So wet for me. You want this cock?" he asks, kissing me on the lips. He sucks my bottom lip into his mouth then releases it, searching my eyes for the answer.

I smile up at him. "Fuck, yeah, I do," I whisper.

He repositions himself at my entrance, and with a flex of his hips, he's inside me. Deep. Stretching. Filling. "So fucking tight," he groans.

It is tight because I wince when the bite of pain becomes almost too much.

King stills. "What's wrong?"

"It's just been a while," I explain.

"I can stop," he says, pulling back slightly.

I dig my nails into his shoulders. "No, you fucking won't," I hear myself growl. "I just need a second."

King chuckles. "There's my girl."

I flex my hips to test my readiness, and he hisses between his teeth. I feel strong, powerful for being able to elicit that kind of reaction from him. "I'm good," I tell him. The truth is that I'm more than good. I'm fucking great. His cock is touching every part of my fucking pussy that needs to be touched, and it's happening all at once. I'm so incredibly full of him, but all I can think is that I want more. So much more. Of this. Of him.

Of us.

King kisses my neck and works his lips up to my jaw, still not moving. "Fuck. I hate that you're not comfortable, but holy fucking shit, you're so tight, you're choking my cock."

"I can stop," I repeat his words, cocking an eyebrow up at him.

Now, it's his turn to use my words against me. "No, you fucking won't," he says with a smirk.

I flex my hips again, and his eyes darken. He begins to move in and out. Each movement eliciting a gasp or moan from either of us. I lift my hips, and he thrusts faster and faster. I keep up the best I can. He's not just fucking me. We're fucking each other.

It's like when fire and ice collide. A bomb of feelings. Opposites coming together in an explosion of the senses. All I can feel, smell, taste, is him. All around me. Inside me. He's everywhere. My body. My heart.

"I'm close. So fucking. close," I manage to cry out.

"I know. I can fucking feel it," King replies, the chords of his neck strained. The muscles of his chest and abs flexing as he thrusts into me over and over again.

My breasts feel heavy, and my skin is on fire. The sound of our bodies slapping together and the smell of sweat and sex is too fucking much. My pussy clamps down around his cock. I convulse, squeezing him with all I have as I come even harder than I had the first time, my vision turning to static and my body lost to the pleasure and feeling and sensations of King. I'm still coming, awash in a wave of a next level orgasm when he places a hand other underneath me, lifting my hips. The other finds its way around my throat. He leaves it there as I feel his cock swell within me, growing even harder until a few wild and lust crazed thrusts later he's groaning my name. My fingers dig into his ass, and he stills as he comes deep within me. "Fuck, Pup. Oh, fuuuuccck," he cries, as he rides my pussy until his own orgasm ebbs and we're left in a pile of sweat and heavy breathing beside each other on the bed.

"I fucking missed that," I say, still trying to catch my breath.

He grabs my chin and forces me to face him. His green eyes staring into mine with a possessive ferocity that I feel in my already heaving chest.

"I fucking missed *you*. All of you. Not just this." His voice grows quiet. I'm feeling every emotion possible for this man, but the loudest of the emotions screaming from within my heart is love.

Always love.

"You scared me for a while there. Don't be afraid to talk to me. Not ever. This is too important. *We* are too important."

I nod. "I didn't want you to think I was weak," I finally admit.

He cradles me in his arms. "Weak? Because you're going through a rough patch? You think what you did by saving Max was weak? You think delivering your own kid is weak? You think by trying to be the hero in our everyday lives while walking around with this internal burden is weak? Pup, you're the strongest fucking person I know. We're in this life together."

I nod and allow him to press me into his chest where my tears soak his already damp skin. "Together," I repeat.

"When you're feeling weak, I'll be strong for you. If you can't see, I'll be your eyes. If you can't hear, I'll guide you. We're only weak when we're not a team. Together? We're un-fucking-stoppable."

My heart constricts in my chest. "You take my breath away."

King holds my gaze. "You are my fucking breath."

CHAPTER 10

RAY

ALTHOUGH KING and I are legally married and bonded to each other in every way, today is our wedding day.

It will be a simple affair that will take place in a field on the farm where Nine and Preppy operate their weed business. Twinkling lights and picnic tables. A no-frills affair followed by a party with friends, family, and a buffet catered by Billy's Crab Shack.

I watch the scenery of Logan's Beach pass by through the window from the backseat of Preppy's Cadillac. He insisted that he and Dre drive me to the wedding, and I couldn't deny him when he seemed so honored to be the one to bring me to King on our wedding day.

I smooth out my dress and pull it out from where it's trapped between the back of my legs and the seat to avoid wrinkles. I dress to avoid it wrinkling. It's not white but blush. No lace or beading for me, just spaghetti straps with a low V in the front, then straight all the way to the floor. I loved it the second I saw it and knew it was what I wanted to marry King in. My platinum hair is straight and parted down the middle with a crown of small flowers that match the color of my dress. The only sparkle is the rose gold leaves surrounding the flowers. Dre did my makeup, and although it's heavier than I normally wear, especially around my eyes, it's still me, just a dolled-up version.

Preppy pokes his head between the front seats and smiles. "You ready for today, kid?"

"Been ready," I reply.

He winks and cuts the engine.

He opens the door for Dre, then runs back around the car to open my door. He's wearing a tan colored tux with a blush pink bow-tie, and I realize why he insisted on seeing my dress the day I bought it.

Preppy offers one arm to Dre and one to me. He leads me around the small one-story office building, and when we round the corner, I stop and unhook my arm from Preppy's to cover my mouth with my hand.

I'm shocked at what I see before me. There are no simple twinkle lights hanging from the trees or picnic table benches lining an unlined aisle.

It's a carnival.

And not a small one either.

It's complete with spinning rides, games with prizes hanging above the carnival workers calling out the low chances to win, and best of all...there's a Ferris wheel.

"What? When? How?" I ask, unable to form a coherent question.

Preppy takes my arm again and leads me forward. "King. It's all King."

King recreated the carnival.

I have happy tears in my eyes as he leads me and Dre to a tent set up in the back. "You look beautiful," Dre says, unhooking her arm from Preppy's. "I'll see you both inside." She ducks inside.

"I'm sorry your pops couldn't be here."

My happiness is temporarily replaced by the sting of not having my dad here. He's recovering from pneumonia and the trip was just too much. Although I did video chat with him after I got ready, so he got to see me in my wedding dress, and he insisted I make sure someone videos the ceremony so he can watch it later.

"It's okay. These things happen."

Preppy shoves his hands in his pockets and rocks on his heels. "So, what would you say if I offered to stand in to substitute."

"I..." I sniffle. "I would like that very much.

His smile beams bright. "I know I'm not your first choice to walk you down the aisle, but sometimes, the second one can surprise you. Like your second choice in an orgy."

I burst out laughing. The music starts to play, and Preppy pushes the tantalizer flap aside. My laughing ceases, and my heart stops when I see King waiting for me at the end of the aisle.

He doesn't take his eyes from me. So much passes between our locked gazes. Love. Lust. History. Future. And although the seats all around us are full of people, it's just me and him in this moment.

I don't even realize the minister is speaking until it's King's turn to recite our vows. We opted to say our own straight from the heart, and I'm leaning toward him, eager to hear what he's chosen to say.

He clears his throat and takes my hands. "I promise to guard this thing between us just like I guard you and the kids. I promise to protect it with my life. Forever."

I'm so full of every emotion that I can't even remember what it was I wanted to say. I sniffle. "How the hell am I supposed to follow that?"

King's eyes never leave mine. "Just promise you'll be mine forever."

"I am yours. Forever. I promise."

"Damn fucking right, you are," King growls. He reaches for me, lifting me up in the air and pressing his lips to mine in a kiss that wouldn't be appropriate for any kind of church wedding.

The crowd hoots and hollers as the reverend closes his book. "I guess you won't be needing the rest of it since you've seem to have taken matters into your own hands. So, by the power vested in me and the fact that you're already legally married, I now pronounce you man and wife."

We're all searching for a little light in the darkness. Something to cling to when life lashes out. I have that with my kids. With King. I make another vow to myself. To trust the safety net he's built around us and lean against him when I feel myself falling. Because King isn't just my husband or my partner, he's my soul, my safe place.

My shelter from any storm.

CHAPTER 11

KING

"YOU MIGHT WANT to take the fucking sign down," Bear says, pointing at the top of the old hunter's shack hidden in amongst the thick pines of Motherfucker Island at the bright neon sign hanging above the door.

Preppy looks up and scratches his head. "Why? Not big enough? Should I have used a 'g' instead of the apostrophe? I knew I shouldn't have gone with slang. ING would have been so much classier."

Bear slaps him in the back of the head. "Because it's a big fuckin' neon sign that says The Killin' Shed."

"How will the people we killin' going to know it's a killin' shed if there's no sign?"

"They will know, and so will the cops," Bear points out, dropping his bag at his feet.

"You two bicker like old ladies at the supermarket fighting over the last of the fucking tapioca," I mumble, adjusting my own heavy leather bag, hanging over my shoulders.

The blue-hairs ignore me and continue on with Preppy

pointing to the sign. "No, they would never think that a place with a sign that says *killin' shed* is an actual killin' shed. Duh, Bear, it's common reverse psychology. Or don't you have books at your big bad biker playhouse?"

"Clubhouse," Bear growls, staying behind with me as Preppy goes inside. The door shuts behind him, but we can still hear him singing. "Ain't no business like Killin' Shed business like no business I knoooowww."

"You know," Bear says, taking a drag off his smoke. "He may have come back to life, but I think some pieces of his fucking brain are still dead."

"Wouldn't be Preppy if we weren't constantly questioning his lack of sanity."

"Ain't that the fucking truth," Bear says. He stubs out his smoke, and we go inside where Preppy is still singing his song while pulling on a pair of thick rubber gloves. The kind meant for welders. Or in our case, murderers.

"Welcome to the killin' shed!" Preppy announces. "It's like Disney World, except there's no rides, and it's not the happiest place on earth. Well, not for you, anyway." Preppy scratches his head. "Shit, I guess it's nothing like Disney World. Okay. Okay. Let me try again." He scratches his chin with the long sharp blade in his hand. "Okay, how about this one." He clears his throat. "Welcome to the killin' shed. The last place you'll ever be."

The guy moans from behind his gag, and Preppy twists his lips. "No? Damn. I'll keep working on it. Too bad you won't get to hear what kind of amazing tag-line I finally do come up with." He taps the knife on the guy's nose. "In case I didn't make it clear, you won't hear it 'cause you'll be all dead and shit." Preppy makes his best dead man hanging at the end of a noose face.

"I think he gets it," Bear says, pointing to the man's pants where a large wet stain has formed. "He pissed himself."

"Oh, goodie. I didn't even have to break out the power point presentation," Preppy says, sauntering back to the table of torture items he's set up, then nods to me. "You're up, bossman."

I don't move because I'm staring at one of the men responsible for the almost deaths of my wife and daughter and the rage courses through my ears and the tunnel vision surrounding his face is all I can concentrate on. "So, you wanted to fuck with the King of the Causeway?" I finally ask. "You're about to feel what happens to people who mess with the wrong fucking family."

Bear takes the knife from Preppy and hands it to me. I test the sharpness of the blade on my fingertips as I slowly walk around the man.

"Any last words?" Bear asks.

The man nods, and I rip the tape from his mouth. "I...I'm sorry. I just want to say...it wasn't my fault."

"Then tell me who," I demand.

"I can't. Anything you do to me here, he'll do worse. He knows where my family lives. That's the way he works with everyone. Nobody will tell you who he is, or they risk losing everything. I can tell you that it he said something about someone named Pike. That all this is because of him. That's all I can tell you." His eyes meet mine. "You know, besides go fuck yourselves."

I cover his mouth back with the tape.

Pike? What the fuck does this have to do with Pike?

"Those were a lot of last fucking *words*," Bear says with a shrug.

"You've been found guilty of high treason," Preppy tells him. "And your sentence is death."

I slice his throat in one swift motion. Blood sprays out and then oozes down his neck. The garbling sounds he makes before his eyes glaze over are annoying as fuck. The guy couldn't even die without pissing me off.

"Shit," Preppy says. He's staring at the blood pooling on the clear plastic covering the floor.

"You going soft?" I ask, wiping the blood from my cheek with my forearm and tossing the knife to the ground.

He rolls his eyes and points a finger at his own chest. "Me? Please. This shit makes my fucking dick hard."

"Then, what's your damage?" Bear asks, lighting a cigarette and testing the electric buzz saw.

"It's that I just remembered that Doc asked me to pick up a tomato sauce on the way home because she'll be back today, and she wants to make...I don't know, something with tomato sauce, and I almost forgot." He eyes the fresh corpse and smiles. "Until now." He pats my shoulder with his thick rubber glove. "Thanks for the reminder, Boss-man."

"Being back here sure reminds me of old times," Bear says, peeling off his gloves. "I miss those days."

"Yeah, the killin' shed has a way of bringing out the best in all of us," Preppy says with what I can only describe as a dreamy sigh, and I swear there's a tear in his fucking eye.

"Today, I agree with you," I reply, lighting a smoke.

"Wanna kill him again?" Preppy asks, picking the knife off the floor.

"Nah," I point to the far side of the room at the other

gagged men with horrified expressions on their doomed faces who just witnessed what their brief futures are going to look like. "We've got two more."

"This is like Christmas, but better and without all the kinky sex," Preppy laments.

Bear's face twists in confusion. "What the fuck kind of Christmases are you having at your house?"

Preppy lets out an exasperated sigh. "Ones with kinky sex. Didn't I just say that?"

Bear and I exchange the same *we're never really going to know where his head is at and it's best not to try* glances.

Preppy points at Bear with his knife. "You going deaf in your old age, Beary-poo?"

"With half the shit you say?" Bear scoffs. "I fucking wish."

Preppy picks up a chainsaw. "Oh, that gives me a good idea. We should cut off their ears."

"Let's just stick to good old fashioned killin', for old time's sake," I say. "Bear, you wanna do the honors?"

Bear plucks the knife from Preppy's hand. "With pleasure."

Preppy huffs. "Always a bridesmaid…"

I slap him on the shoulder. "You get the next one, Prep."

His frown turns into a beaming smile. He revs the chainsaw and shouts over the deafening sound. "Like I said, just like fucking Christmas."

Find out more about the mystery man causing problems in Logan's Beach in Pike's book. Coming 2020. Keep reading for a preview.

A QUICK NOTE

In the US, one out of every nine new mothers will suffer from Postpartum depression. PPD can affect any mom, regardless of her age, ethnicity, marital status, number of kids, or income. [1]It can last for weeks, months or years.

14-23% of women will experience some form of depression during pregnancy.

Most importantly, it's nobody's fault.

Postpartum depression and depression during pregnancy are as real as any other kind of depression. I know because I lived through it. There were nights when I would sit on the floor of my baby's room next to her crib and quietly cry for hours. I couldn't leave the house for weeks because even the smallest of tasks, like what to dress the baby in or even myself for a trip to the grocery store, or packing the stroller into the car, completely overwhelmed me.

The term 'baby blues' is adorable, but I assure you there's nothing adorable about the way it makes you feel.

I need you to do something for me. If you know someone

who has recently had a baby, give them a call. *Today.* Ask them how they're doing. Most likely, they're going to say they're fine, or maybe, that they're *just tired*.

When they do, ask them how they're *really* doing. It can make all the difference to someone suffering.

If you or someone you know is suffering from depression, please seek help.

A PREVIEW OF PIKE

MICKEY

Mom and Dad always beam with pride when they tell people I have a photographic memory, even though the accomplishment is the least spectacular among those of my three younger sisters. Mallory, the youngest at thirteen, is already on the junior Olympic swim team. Maya, sixteen, recently received her early acceptance letter to Stanford. Mindy, seventeen, paints spectacular watercolor landscapes and landed her first solo gallery show in Miami next month.

Then, there's me. Micky, nineteen, photographic memory.

Eh, seems pale in comparison.

I hear my Dad's voice in my head at dinner last month with my aunt and uncle. *"Bob, did I ever tell you that Micky here has a photographic memory. It's astounding. She can remember every detail of everything she sees. Never seen anything like it. Bob, give me your driver's license. She'll remember the numbers in two-seconds flat."*

I chuckle to myself at the image of Bob's astonished face

when I did just that, taking a quick glance at his driver's license before handing it back and reciting not just his license number, but his birthday, the date he got his license renewed, and the fact that he's an organ donor. I added the part about him having a ketchup stain on his collar in the picture for good measure.

My memory has always been my super power. It's never failed me.

My smile falls.

Until, today.

Today, Dad's brag is a lie.

Because something happened today, and for the first time in my life, I can't remember what.

The memory is there, but it's sitting inside my brain like a shredded picture floating in the wind. Just when I feel like I'm getting close to it, it's gone again. It's like catching something moving in the corner of your eye only to turn around and realize that nothing's there.

It's as if I'm chasing ghosts.

The sound of my sisters' laughter brings me back to the present. I brush off the uneasy feeling and plaster a bright smile on my face.

Whatever happened must not have been that important. Because if it was, I'm sure I'd remember. Because it's who I am. I'm the daughter who remembers.

Whatever is going on with my memory is going to have to wait, because I refuse to let anything bother me, especially not here, my happy place.

My family and I vacation here in Logan's Beach every summer. We have a small timeshare right on the beach. All of my greatest memories took place in this town. I lost my first tooth here. I had my first kiss on the pier. Even though the kiss was as gross as whatever was stuck in Hudson Yontz's braces, the memory still makes me smile. My mom taught me how to swim in the pool of the timeshare here. My sisters and I even won a fishing tournament here. We called our team the Snook Sisters, and that year, the Snook Sisters took home first place. You would have thought we'd won the lottery instead of a forty-five-dollar gift certificate to Master Bait & Tackle.

The warmth of the sun begins to cool and the unrelenting heat fades from the back of my neck leaving a cool spot in its place as the breeze brushes across my wet skin.

I glance up to the sky and notice the sun dropping into the horizon.

Sunset already? Where did the time go? Didn't we just leave the timeshare to go kayaking a few minutes ago?

We did. That I remember. We packed up the van. Strapped the kayaks to the roof. Stopped to buy more sunscreen.

And then...nothing.

I brush the thought off again.

I mean time always flies by during our summers here. It's not that unusual for me to lose track of it.

But not of your memory.

I refuse to enter into that line of conversation again with my inner voice. After all, it hasn't gotten me anywhere so far.

The sign that says *Welcome to Logan's Beach* glows green under the fading light as I approach it. Every week during the summer, there's either a large black spray-painted dick across the lettering, or a patch of wet paint.

Today, it's wet paint.

I smile to myself as I slowly walk past the sign. My feet ache from walking. Always the drama queen, I hear Mallory complaining about hers behind me, and I roll my eyes.

My Mom assures her we are almost there. I almost ask where there is, but I don't want to ruin the summer with them worrying about me. Instead, I listen as Dad tells a bad knock-knock joke that makes my sisters and my mom simultaneously groan, but I can't help the little giggle that escapes my mouth.

Mindy chides me for encouraging my Dad and groans even louder when he starts telling another joke. But I don't mind because even Dad's jokes are more tolerable in Logan's Beach.

Everything is sweeter here. Better.

Even sharing a bathroom with my three sisters is more tolerable here then it is at home, and the one at home at least has two sinks where the one in the timeshare only has one.

As we walk, I'm leaving a snail-like trail of water on the pavement behind me. My clothes have gone from wet to damp under the heat of the sun, my jeans shorts chafing the inside of my thighs as they rub the skin raw with each step, but my wild mass of hair is like a deranged sponge and once it's wet, it leaks like a runny faucet until I can find a towel and a blow dryer because air drying is not an option.

Maya notices my wet trail and jokes that I should be one of those Sham-wow infomercials. Not as the salesperson shouting about how fabulous the water absorbent cloth is, but as the cloth itself.

"Like I haven't heard that one before," I mutter.

Mom tells her to be nice, and I smile and stick my tongue out.

Dad tells us all to stop walking and take in salty air.

Normally, I'd roll my eyes or just pretend to go along with it, but it's my last summer here before I head to college, and who knows, maybe my last summer here ever, and I made a promise to myself that I'm going to savor each and every minute I have left in this place so I do what Dad says and stop, face the water, and close my eyes. The salt is so thick in the air that I can taste it in my mouth before I even have a chance to inhale.

When I do try and take a deep breath, I can't. My lungs are already full, but it's not of air. I cough one of those gross wet coughs where you can feel stuff moving around in your lungs. And the air really is like a salt lick because what I do cough up tastes like I've been licking one all day.

My mother comes to my side to ask if I'm okay. I nod wipe my mouth with the back of my hand and flash her a smile, reassuring her that I'm fine. She reminds me that I always get a cold at the end of the summer. She's right. I always do.

I smirk to myself. Mallory will be wearing her surgical mask the entire trip home so she doesn't catch my cold. She'll be giving me her usual raised eyebrow side glances every time I sneeze like I've got the zombie plague. I make a mental note to throw in some additional fake sneezes and coughs for good measure.

We continue walking, and I realize that my feet are aching to the point that I'm limping. I do my best to hide it so Mom won't worry. I don't want to complain either, she's heard enough of those today. Besides, she said we're almost there, so I'll be able to rest them soon.

The white and yellow of approaching headlights spread wide in the light of dawn like portals of blurry suns. I pause and shield my eyes for a moment before we all continue on. A horn blasts loud from a passing car, making Maya jump and Mallory curse as it fades off down the road.

After a few more miles, the road becomes thin and cracked with no marking separating the lanes. There are no more lights or bars or people.

Mindy whines to my Dad, and he assures her again that we are almost there, but I'm beginning to think *there* doesn't exist.

A black truck pulls up beside us and stops. It's on big lifted tires. I crane my neck when the window rolls down. A man appears although he's so high up I can't make out his face.

"Miss, you need a ride?" he asks, sounding concerned.

I smile and my lips crack, a trickle of blood runs down my jaw, and I wipe it away with my wet shirt. It stings from the salt but my smile doesn't falter.

All three of my sisters are begging my parents to let us get into this stranger's truck, but I know they'll never allow it so as much as I appreciate the offer, I politely decline.

"Thank you so much, but no thank you."

My sisters giggle, and although I can't see the man, I realize that he must be cute because my sisters are giggling like idiots.

I whip my head around. "Shhh, don't be rude," I say between my teeth and turn back to the stranger. "Sorry about them."

"Them," he says, as if he doesn't understand why young women would be giggling in his presence. I might be, too, but his face is even blurrier now than it was when he first pulled up. In fact, everything is blurrier now.

We need to keep going so we can get there. "Thanks again

for the offer," I say to the man, "but as you can see, even if we were to take you up on your kind offer, your truck doesn't have a backseat, and I don't think it can accommodate all six of us."

"All six of you," he repeats. It's not a statement or a question.

My feet ache, and I'm shifting from one to the other. I'm eager to send this stranger on his way because I'm finding it harder and harder to remain upright. "Yeah, you don't think I'd leave my family here and go with you alone, did you?" I ask. I turn back to my Dad and shoot him a shrug. He smiles proudly, no doubt at the realization that his constant stranger-danger talks have sunk in.

"Miss, where is your family?" he asks, tentatively.

I frown. I mean, my vision is blurry but this man must be downright blind.

"Right behind me!" I wave my arms to where my family is gathered at the side of the road. They wave back.

He opens the driver's door and hops down onto the pavement. I register bare arms and a white shirt, but not much else.

I don't know if it's the sudden movement or the long walk that has me swaying on my feet.

The man glances over my shoulder into the dark, then back at me before repeating the process again. His facial features look like a close-up image of a fly. Large and nonsensical. He scratches his head in confusion.

I growl in frustration and spin around to point my family out to him, but the movement continues even as my body stops. Everything spins. My family. The truck. The stranger. The moon above me. Faster and faster like an out of control carnival ride.

I catch one last glimpse of my family as I fall.

The last words I hear before I hit the ground are deep and garbled.

"Miss...there ain't nobody behind you."

Want to read more of Pike's story? CLICK HERE

ALSO BY T.M. FRAZIER

THE PERVERSION TRILOGY
PERVERSION (Book 1)

POSSESSION (Book 2)

PERMISSION (Book 3)

THE OUTSKIRTS DUET
THE OUTSKIRTS (Book 1)

THE OUTLIERS (Book 2)

THE KING SERIES
LISTED IN RECOMMENDED READING ORDER

Jake & Abby's Story (Standalone)

The Dark Light of Day (Prequel)

King & Doe's Story (Duet)

KING (Book 1)

TYRANT (Book 2)

Bear & Thia's Story (Duet)

LAWLESS (Book 3)

SOULLESS (Book 4)

Rage & Nolan's Story (Standalone)
ALL THE RAGE (Spinoff)

Preppy & Dre's Story (Triplet)
PREPPY PART ONE (Book 5)
PREPPY PART TWO (Book 6)
PREPPY PART THREE (Book 7)

Smoke & Frankie's Story (Standalone)
UP IN SMOKE (Spinoff)

Nine & Lenny's Story
NINE, THE TALE OF KEVIN CLEARWATER

Pike's Story (Duet)
Pike (Book 1)
Pawn (Book 2)

ABOUT THE AUTHOR

T.M. Frazier never imagined that a single person would ever read a word she wrote when she published her first book, The Dark Light of Day.

Now, she's a USA Today bestselling author several times over. Her books have been translated into numerous languages and published all around the world.

T.M. enjoys writing what she calls 'wrong side of the tracks' romance with sexy, morally corrupt anti-heroes and ballsy heroines.

Her books have been described as raw, dark and gritty. Basically, while some authors are great at describing a flower as it blooms, T.M. is better at describing it in the final stages of decay.

She loves meeting her readers, but if you see her at an event please don't pinch her because she's not ready to wake up from this amazing dream.

For more information please visit her website www.tmfrazierbooks.com

FACEBOOK: facebook.com/tmfrazierbooks
TWITTER: twitter.com/tm_frazier
INSTAGRAM: instagram.com/t.m.frazier
JOIN MY FACEBOOK GROUP, FRAZIERLAND: www.facebook.com/groups/tmfrazierland

Printed in Great Britain
by Amazon